THE COMBATIVE

THE COMBATIVE

THE ELIMINATOR SERIES BOOK 10

MIKE RYAN

WWW.MIKERYANBOOKS.COM

1

J acobs was throwing a tennis ball across the yard with Gunner retrieving it. In between throws, Jacobs moved his arm around and leaned over to stretch out his side. It'd been two months since the last incident with Ames' crew at the apartment complex. He was basically healed, but had been keeping a low profile since then. Besides taking the time to heal, he also didn't want to re-engage with Ames' bunch until he was a hundred percent. Or at least close to it.

Jacobs had just thrown another ball and was waiting for Gunner to come back with it, when Tiffany appeared by the back door. Their relationship had grown over the past couple of months, with the two of them getting closer, though they hadn't really taken the next step. With Ames knowing where she lived and where she worked, Jacobs was worried about her going back to her apartment alone. So when he proposed that she stayed with him for a while, at least until he was sure it was safe for her to live by herself again, it didn't really take a lot to convince her. And Jacobs didn't even mind taking her to and from work every day. It almost made them feel like a real couple, even though they hadn't reached that step yet.

Tiffany went into the backyard, and Gunner ran up to her with the ball. She took it out of his mouth and threw it again. Her staying there was also helped by the fact that Gunner really took to her.

"How are you feeling?"

"Good," Jacobs replied.

"I was watching you from the window, and I saw you moving your arm."

"It's fine. I was just making sure my motion was still good. It wasn't because I was in pain."

"OK. I'll trust you."

They stood there for a few more minutes, alternating between who was throwing the ball to Gunner. Finally, Tiffany said what was on her mind.

"You know, not that I've minded being here with you, because I haven't. It's been really great."

"I feel a but coming on."

"But I can't stay here forever. I'm eventually going to have to go back to my own place. Or find a new one."

The truth was that Jacobs was starting to get used to her being around. Even though they hadn't taken that next step, he really didn't want her to leave.

"Um, you don't have to leave anytime soon if you

don't want to. I mean, I'm not kicking you out or anything."

Tiffany smiled. "I know. And believe me, I've enjoyed staying here. You're great. I love Gunner. But this isn't my home. And nothing's happened in the last two months."

"Doesn't mean nothing won't."

"Brett, you can't protect me forever."

"Why not?"

Tiffany huffed. "Brett, you can't do this to yourself."

"Do what?"

"Beat yourself up. What happened to me wasn't your fault."

"It was. Everything has always been my fault. The decisions I've made have put other people's lives in danger. Including yours. I knew being around you was a mistake. I knew it was dangerous for you. And I let it happen anyway."

Tiffany looked down. She wasn't able to hide the disappointment in his words. "Being around me was a mistake, huh?"

"That's not what I meant."

"Well, maybe I should just mistake my way out of your life. You can pretend I never existed."

Tiffany turned around swiftly and began storming off. Jacobs quickly raced in front of her to stop her. He put his hands on her arms and looked into her eyes. "Hey. You know that's not what I meant."

"Isn't it?"

"No. It's not. Being around you, when I'm with you, I feel like I can be the person I used to be. Like I'm not carrying around fifty pounds of guilt on my back." Jacobs looked away from her for a second and wiped one of his eyes to prevent them from tearing up. "But I can't let that interfere with the fact that bad things happen to people who know me. Some people, like Eddie, are willing to accept those risks."

"And what makes you think I'm not?"

"Because you shouldn't have to. What happened to you is something that should have never happened. And it's not something you should ever have to worry about."

"So why do I have to?"

"What?"

"Brett, there's nothing keeping you here." Jacobs tilted his head back, trying to understand what she was getting at. It didn't take long for her to make it crystal clear. "You're here because you choose to be. You don't have to stay here and worry about any of this. You could move somewhere else, start a new life, and not have to worry about any of this ever again. But you stay here and constantly put yourself in danger."

Jacobs didn't really have an answer for her. At least not a good one. "I don't know. Maybe because my family's here. This is where I'm from. I've always been here."

"That doesn't mean you have to be glued here no matter what. And your family will be with you no matter where you go. You don't have to give up their memories. They'll always be with you."

"I know, but..."

"You've got this notion inside of you that you can never be happy again. That you don't deserve to be. But you can. You can move on. I'm not asking you to forget. But you can choose to be happy again. But you have to let yourself."

Jacobs tried to smile, but it wasn't much of one. "I guess it's just hard to let go."

"You have to want to. And so far, you haven't. Maybe I'm not the right person to help you with that. But somewhere out there, someone is. And I hope you find them."

Tiffany tried to walk past him again, but he grabbed her arm once more, spinning her around to face him.

Jacobs gently held her arm. "Don't go."

"Why not?"

"Because I don't want you to."

"Brett, you can't have your cake and eat it too."

"I hate that saying."

"But it's true. You know what I want. It's the same thing I've wanted since I met you. But you're not ready for that. And that's fine. I understand. I'm not mad. But being here with you for the past two months has been..."

"What?"

Tiffany looked away for a second. "It's been nice.

And it's only reinforced that I can't have what I want. And that's you." She wiped a tear from her eye. "And I wish things were different. I wish you were ready. But you're not. Or maybe you are. Maybe I'm just not the one who can help you get there."

Jacobs turned and looked at Gunner for a second, who was lying on the grass, watching the two of them argue. With his concentration elsewhere, Tiffany was finally able to slip by him. Jacobs turned back around and saw Tiffany heading inside the house again. He quickly ran after her. As she entered the kitchen, Jacobs grabbed her arm again.

"What is it that you want from me?"

Tiffany stared into his eyes. "Do you really need to ask that question?"

"I'm just supposed to pick up and leave and go somewhere else? And do what?"

Tiffany threw her arms up. "I don't know. You can do anything you want. You could get a regular job. You could start your own business. You could work in security. You could do just about anything you wanted. You have experience. You could make it work if you tried."

"And if I went to Cleveland, or Detroit, or Atlanta, or wherever, you would just come with me? Just like that?"

"If it was what you really wanted."

"You would just follow me?"

"Well, I'm not gonna follow you around like a little lost puppy, hoping that you eventually throw me a bone. But if you truly wanted to make a new life, something that we could create together, and you actually wanted me, then yes, I would go with you. But Brett, I'm not Valerie. I can never be. And I can't replace her. And I would never try. All I can do is be me. And hope that that's enough." Her eyes started tearing up again.

"It is."

Tears fell down both her cheeks. She wiped them away. "But it's not. Not yet. You still carry that pain around. You're not ready to let someone in yet. And I'm not gonna try to force you. And I'm not gonna try to pressure you. I told you when we met that I'd never do that."

Gunner came into the room and barked. Jacobs looked at him. "Stay out of it." He looked back at Tiffany. "Say I did decide to go somewhere else. What would you do about your job? You love those kids."

Tiffany got her tears under control again. "I do. And I would never leave them in the middle of a school year or anything. But there are teaching jobs available in other places. I could put my name in. And if there's nothing available right away, I could always get put on the sub list first and work my way in. There are options. But it's not about me. If *we* decided it was the right thing to do, we could figure out a way to make it work. We can plan. We can figure it out. But *you* have to decide it's what you really want."

"I'm just not sure I can leave yet."

"Why? What else is holding you here? It's not just your family."

Jacobs sighed and ran his hand over his head, scratching and rubbing it. "With Ames running around..."

"Stop. Just stop. Why does that even matter to you?"

"Why? I can't just let him do what he did and let him get away with it. I'm supposed to just walk away from it?"

Tiffany nodded. "Yeah. Just walk away. Why do you need to get revenge on him? Why do you need to be the one who brings him down? You're not a cop anymore. He's not your problem. Let the police worry about him."

"I'm not sure I can do that."

"You can. You just won't. Brett, he's not the one who murdered your family. He had nothing to do with that. You choosing to stay here and fight him has nothing to do with your past or not being able to let go. That's just you staying here because you want to. Not because you feel you have to. He didn't kill your family."

"But he tried to hurt you."

"If I can let it go and move on, then so should you." Jacobs made a face that indicated he wasn't sure what else to say. "It's OK. Like I said, I'm not mad. You're not ready to move on. Believe me, I completely understand. I guess I'm just venting a bit, but I'm not angry. I get it. You wanna take your pain out and unleash it on every bad guy you come across. It's just the way it is right now. And I'm not saying I want you out of my life or that we can never talk again. But I just can't keep living here with you. It's time for me to go back."

Tiffany turned and headed for the door, but Jacobs raced back in front of her again.

"No."

Tiffany folded her arms. "What do you mean, no?"

"I mean no. I can't..." Jacobs looked around, hoping the right words would come to him. "I can't let you go back to your apartment, not knowing if something bad is happening to you. I can't lose you too."

"Then what do you suggest?"

"I don't know. Just let me think about it."

"We've had two months to think about it."

"I know. Just give me a few more days to come up with something that'll work for both of us. You won't have to be tormented staying here with me, and I won't have to worry about you every second that we're not together." Tiffany clenched her jaw tighter, and he could see that she wasn't completely happy with his suggestion. "Please, just give me two more days. I care about you. And I wanna make sure that you're safe. Just a couple more days."

Tiffany sighed. "Fine. Two more days."

Jacobs grinned. "Thank you."

Some of the steam was starting to evaporate from Tiffany's system. She looked at the time. "I guess I'm gonna go make myself something for lunch. Would you like something?"

Jacobs shrugged. "I guess that depends."

"On what?"

"Were you planning on letting me eat it or were you going to throw it at me?"

She chuckled. "Don't give me ideas. But I guess I'll let you eat this one."

Jacobs smiled. "Then yeah, I guess I could eat something. Thank you."

Tiffany turned and walked into the kitchen to make them something to eat. After she disappeared from sight, Jacobs looked down, observing Gunner still staring at him.

"What?" Gunner let out a bark. "I know what I'm doing." Gunner growled. "Yeah. I hope so too."

2

_____

Jacobs went over to the door and looked through the peephole just to make sure it was who he was expecting. He opened it, allowing Franks to come in.

"Hey, what's going on?"

Jacobs shrugged. "Same old, same old."

Franks nodded. "I hear ya, man, I hear ya." He looked around. He didn't see Tiffany or Gunner. "Where's the pooch at, man?"

"The pooch is outside."

"Oh. How about the old lady? The old ball and chain?"

"The what?"

"Tiffany. Where she at?"

"The old ball and chain?"

Franks laughed and backhanded Jacobs in the

front of his shoulder. "Just a little play on words there, you know?"

"Uh, I guess."

"That's how they used to refer to a person's other half way back in the day, you know," Franks said.

"It is, huh?"

"Oh yeah. So where's she?"

"She's out with the pooch."

Franks laughed again. "That dog loves her."

"Yeah."

Franks stared at Jacobs' face for a few seconds. Jacobs stared back, raising an eyebrow, wondering what was going on. Franks was intently studying his friend's facial expression.

"What are we doing here?" Jacobs asked.

Franks slowly formed a smile. "Why you sly dog, you."

"What?"

"You went and done it, didn't you?"

"I did what?"

"You went and got back on the horse, didn't you?"

Jacobs sighed and shook his head. "Why do you always wind up resorting to metaphors that I can't understand?"

"It's my style, man. And really, I'd think you'd know what I'm talking about by now. I mean, we've known each other forever and a day."

Jacobs rubbed his forehead. "Sure feels like a lot longer than that."

Franks slapped Jacobs on the arm again, seeming pretty happy. "I'm proud of you, man."

Jacobs held his arm. "Can you watch it there? I am recovering, you know."

"Oh, please, you're as fine as fine can be."

"Glad you think so."

"So gimme the details, man." Franks rubbed his hands together. "Lemme know how it happened."

"How what happened?"

"You getting back in the saddle."

"Would you stop talking like you're an old cowboy and I'm John Wayne or something? What the hell are you talking about?"

"You and Tiff, man."

"Me and Tiff, what?"

Franks moved his arms around, trying to indicate something, though Jacobs was still lost on what. "You know."

Jacobs shook his head. "If you don't tell me exactly what you're talking about in the next ten seconds, I'm leaving."

Franks rolled his eyes and threw his hands up. "You and Tiffany, man. You're back in the game."

Jacobs didn't look happy. "Eddie. This is your last chance to tell me what's going on in that one-of-a-kind mind of yours."

"It's written all over your face, man. You and her finally did it. I mean, you look as happy as I've seen you in a while."

"I do?"

"Yeah. C'mon, give me the details. Did you finally lower your defenses, or did she come on to you? What happened?"

Jacobs shook his head again. "Unbelievable. I have no idea how you've gotten to the place you're in right now, but you couldn't be any farther away than if you were... I don't even know what."

"Say what now?"

"There's nothing on my face that indicates me and Tiffany have done anything close to what you're thinking."

"Really?"

"Why is that so shocking?"

"Because you look all relaxed and happy. I thought for sure you finally sowed your oats again."

"Oh my god, will you please stop talking like that?"

"OK, OK. But you and her didn't do it?"

"No. We didn't."

"Well, that's disappointing. What the hell are you two kids waiting for?"

"Why do you care?"

"Because you're my friend, ain't ya?"

"I suppose so."

"Well, I want you to be happy. And it looked to me like you and her were heading in that direction."

Jacobs shook his head. "We're not."

"What the hell's wrong with you, man?"

"Nothing."

"There's a fine, pretty young thing living in your house for two months, and you haven't done anything about it?"

"Uh, yeah, that's about it."

Franks shook his head and sighed. "Man, are you ever gonna get back on that horse?"

"What'd I tell you about that?"

"OK, fine, whatever. Point blank, man, what the hell is wrong with you?"

"Why does something have to be wrong with me?"

"Because you've been living together for two months, and she's obviously into you, you like her, so I don't understand what the holdup is."

"Because I'm not ready."

Franks put his hand on Jacobs' shoulder and lowered his head, shaking it for a second before looking back up at him. "Then why do you look so relaxed?"

Jacobs shrugged. "Beats me. As a matter of fact, we just had an argument an hour or so ago."

Jacobs then walked away, heading toward the back-yard as if it were no big deal. Franks quickly followed after him. They eventually found themselves on the back deck, leaning on the railing, watching Tiffany play fetch with Gunner. She eventually noticed them standing there and waved, with Franks waving back.

"I dunno, man. Maybe you know what you're doing, but I sure have my doubts about it."

"And what was with all that talk about getting back

in the saddle, anyway?" Jacobs asked. "I've had sex before."

"Yeah, but not since the missus, god rest her soul."

"Are you just forgetting about..."

"Don't even bring up her name, man. Don't even do it. Because I'm just pretending like that whole episode didn't even exist. Besides, she drugged you, knocked you out, tied you up; you didn't even know if you were coming or going. So that don't even count."

"It doesn't, huh?"

"No, it don't. So don't even bring up her name. I don't ever wanna hear about that woman again."

Jacobs finally let out a smile. Franks seemed like he was still more upset about that situation than he was.

"Let's get back to what I called you over here for."

"Oh, yeah. I almost forgot about that. What did you call me over here for, anyway?"

"I need help keeping her safe."

Franks looked at him curiously. "Seems like you've been doing a pretty good job so far."

"Yeah, but she wants to get back to her own place."

"And you're gonna let her?"

"I don't wanna let her. But she's given me two days to find a solution, otherwise she's going back to her old apartment."

"Well, that's not safe."

"I know that. That's why I want you to help figure something out."

"Why can't she just continue to stay here? Why you kicking her out?"

"I'm not kicking her out. I want her to stay," Jacobs said. "But she doesn't want to stay if we're just gonna continue what we're doing."

"So you want your cake and eat it too, huh?"

"Why does everyone keep saying that?"

"You want the benefits of her staying here, but you don't wanna give her the old grease monkey, is that it?"

Jacobs shook his head. "I'm just gonna pretend you didn't say that."

"Say what?"

"Forget it."

"So why can't you just give her what she wants and be done with it?" Franks said.

"Because Ames is still out there. I can't walk away from that."

"You can. You just don't want to."

"Eddie, I just had the same argument with her. And I really don't want to go through it again. And I also don't wanna be lectured about my private life. If I don't wanna move on, that's my business, OK?"

"OK, man, OK."

"Now, do you wanna help keep her safe or don't you?"

"Well, of course I wanna keep her safe, man. What kind of question is that?"

"OK, so help me figure out a way to do that."

"Well, you could let her go back to her old place

and just sit outside her apartment twenty-four seven to make sure she's OK."

"Something practical. I can't just sit outside her apartment all day," Jacobs said.

"Well, you won't have to when she's at work."

"Something practical, Eddie."

"That is practical. Even if you don't wanna do it yourself, you could always hire someone else to do it. Plenty of guys would take that money."

"Money I don't wanna pay."

"Well, you asked."

"Eddie, if you don't have..."

Franks put his hands up. "All right, man, all right, I'm still thinking. Just give me some time." Franks looked at Tiffany again. "You mean to tell me you're not willing to..."

"Focus, Eddie, focus. We've already been through that. No need to do it again."

"Oh. Yeah. Um, let's see. Well, we could set her up in a different place, put it under a different name and all, of course. I mean, that would solve that problem fairly easily. Just give her a fake name and some docs, I mean, we could do that no sweat. But that wouldn't solve the other problem, and that's the big one."

"What's that?"

"Ames knows who she is. That means he knows where she works."

"I know."

"And considering she's not a professional hitman,

she ain't got the training to avoid being followed home from work one day, which means all that planning on a new place will get thrown right out the window."

"I know."

"Of course, there is another solution."

"What's that?"

"We ship her out of town. If she's in a new city, Ames ain't gonna care about her anymore."

Jacobs looked at Tiffany playing with Gunner. "I think that's gonna be a tough sell. I don't think she's got an interest in doing that."

Franks scratched the side of his face as he continued to think. "Well, there's one final thing I can think of at the moment."

"Which is?"

"She stays here."

"Uh, yeah, I think that's gonna be a tough sell too."

"Think about it. The safest place for her right now is here with you."

"I know that."

"You can still take her to work and pick her up."

"I know."

"And you can spot a tail if there is one."

"I know that too."

"And she wouldn't be safer anywhere else," Franks said.

"I know."

"So in my opinion, the safest place for her is to stay here."

"I know that too."

"Well, if you know all this, then what are you asking me for?"

"Because she doesn't know it," Jacobs said.

"Oh. Well, you want me to have a crack at her?"

Jacobs raised an eyebrow. "A what now?"

"Don't be getting dirty on me, man, you know what I meant. I'll have a talk with her."

"If you think you can reach her, be my guest."

"I certainly can't do any worse than you did, huh?"

"No, I guess not."

Franks tapped his friend on the arm. "Let the old master have a shot at her."

"Let me know when he gets here."

"Very funny, man, very funny."

Franks walked down the steps from the deck into the backyard. Gunner went right by him like he wasn't even there.

"Oh, I see how it is now. You got somebody better looking here, and now I get kicked to the curb, is that it?" Tiffany looked at Franks and laughed. Franks kept his attention on Gunner. "You know there used to be a time when I was your number two, man, what happened? Just because she's prettier than I am, and you gotta up and leave me?"

Gunner lay down and barked once at him.

"I see how it is." Tiffany smiled at him. "Hey, Tiff, how you doing today?"

She shrugged. "Same as most days, I guess."

"Brett told me you and he had a bit of a tussle in there."

"It was nothing, really."

"He cares about you, you know."

"I know he does."

"And you care about him?"

"You know I do," Tiffany said.

"Then don't put any added..."

"Eddie, if you're going to tell me that I'm gonna make him more worried or something if I'm living somewhere else, then you're wasting your time. Or if you came to talk me out of leaving, you're also wasting your time."

"Awe, come on, honey, at least let me finish what I came here to say."

Tiffany tilted her head as if she still didn't want to hear it. "Eddie, I like you. You've been nice to me."

"And I like you too. That's why I'm here. I don't wanna see anything happen to you."

"And nothing will."

"You don't know that. The safest place for you to be is right here," Franks said.

"Why is that fair to me? Why do I have to stay someplace where I don't want to be?"

"You don't wanna be here?" Franks gave her a distrustful eye. "Really?"

"Not like this. You know how I feel about him. But I'm not gonna be one of those women who waits years for a breadcrumb."

"And I don't blame you there. I don't. The man is obviously insane and doesn't know what's best for him. But that's why you gotta stay here. So you and I can continue working on him."

"I've been here for two months, Eddie. If he's not worn down by now, he's not gonna be."

"We just need a little bit more time, that's all."

"I don't have any more time to give."

"You couldn't give a few more tough weeks for a possible lifetime of happiness?"

"A few more tough weeks?"

"Just hear me out. How about you give him a few more weeks? A month or two at the most."

"Now it's a month or two?"

"Just until we're able to get rid of Ames. Then the problem will be over," Eddie said.

"Until a new one comes along, and he latches on to that."

"Can you just do me one favor? Just promise me you'll stay here until one of two things happen."

"Which is?"

"Either we find you another place that we know is a hundred and fifty percent safe for you to stay in, or until Ames is gone, whichever is later."

"Whichever is later?"

"Yeah, I mean, these things take time."

"It doesn't take any time for me to go back to my old apartment," she said.

"No, see, that's the wrong thing. Ames' bunch

already know you're there. They took you out of there once already. Are you really gonna feel safe going back there again? I mean, really?"

Tiffany sighed. "I can't keep living like this. I feel like I'm on house arrest with someone who doesn't want to be with me. I mean, it'd be one thing if we were intimate or something, or he showed some type of interest in me, but he doesn't."

Franks nodded, understanding her frustration. "I hear you there. I gotcha. But if you go back to your old place, and something happens, do you really wanna put the both of you back into that situation again?"

"No."

"Now, the only other possibility is... He talked to his old police buddies, and they said they could get you a new identity in another city if that's what you wanted."

"A new identity?"

"Yeah, but that means you could never look back. Never talk to anyone from here again. Now is that what you really want?"

Tiffany looked up at Jacobs, who was sitting down in a chair, looking away from them. She then looked back at Gunner. She then faced Franks again and sighed. "Fine. I'll give you a few more weeks, but that's all. You better figure out another living situation for me, because we both know, he's not changing anytime soon."

Franks gave her a smile. "You're doing the right

thing. I promise you I'll start looking into things. But don't give up hope." He looked up at Jacobs for a second as well. "There's a piece of him in there that wants to go back to his old self. It's a small piece, but it's there. We just have to find it."

3

J acobs strolled across the field on the way to his family's graves. It'd been too long since he'd been there. But with Franks staying with Tiffany for the moment, it seemed like a good time to visit. About halfway there, though, he noticed something strange. There was something on Valerie's grave. Jacobs couldn't quite tell what it was yet, but it was white and looked rectangular. It could've been a piece of paper or an envelope. He couldn't figure out what was holding it to the grave.

As Jacobs got up close, he could see that it was an envelope taped to the grave. He slowly peeled it off and looked at it. It had "Brett Jacobs" written in cursive on the front. He didn't recognize the handwriting. He opened the envelope and removed a small piece of paper that was folded. He unfolded it and read what was written, the letters also in cursive. It simply said, "call," and then a phone number. Jacobs examined both the piece of paper and the envelope. They were both written in the same ink, and though none of the letters matched, it looked like the same type of handwriting. He stared at the phone number for a few moments. He didn't know it. He then took a look around, getting the feeling that he was being watched. Nothing jumped out at him, though it wouldn't have been the first time someone surprised him while he was there.

Jacobs continued spinning in every direction for a few seconds, looking at every tree, every car, every window that was in sight, just waiting for that slight movement that indicated someone was nearby with a gun, pointed right at him. He never saw that movement though. He stood there, still expecting something to happen. When nothing did, he eventually turned his attention back to his family. He put the paper back in the envelope, then put that in his pocket. Jacobs knelt down on one knee and let out a loud sigh.

"I'm sorry it's been so long. It's been... it's been a crazy couple of months. I've still been thinking about you guys every day, though."

Jacobs reached out and touched the grave, wiping off a few pieces of dirt and grass.

"I guess you know what's been going on. I dunno. I don't know what to do anymore. I thought I did. I thought after I got rid of Mallette, that'd be the end for me. I'd avenge what happened to you guys, I'd get my revenge, then I'd come up to join you. I was ready."

Jacobs looked away and sighed again. After a few moments, he turned his attention back to the graves.

"I was ready. Then Ames came along, and then there was something new to fight for, and... I think I kind of lost my way a little bit. But through it all, I still had every intention of joining you."

Jacobs looked away again and wiped his right eye, feeling like a tear was coming on. Getting his emotions under control, he continued talking.

"But now... I don't know. I just really don't know. Now there's Tiffany, and right away, right away, the day I met her in that park, I just knew she was different, you know?"

Both of Jacobs' eyes started tearing up now. He wiped both of them.

"I mean, she's everything you were. Pretty, smart, funny; she's got that warm personality, you know? And I've been trying to push her away, and no matter what I've done, it's come out wrong. I didn't want to get involved, but it happened anyway."

He looked down at the ground and shook his head, getting his emotions in check again.

"I dunno, I guess I didn't try hard enough. Maybe I really didn't want to. Maybe I was hoping for something else, even if I knew it was unlikely. I don't know. I don't know much of anything anymore. I don't know what I want. I don't know what I feel. I just don't know.

It's not fair what's happened to her. What if I let her get closer, and the same thing happens to her that happened to you? I don't know if I could handle it again."

He reached over and swiped a few more pieces of grass off the grave.

"I guess I'm just afraid. Afraid of getting hurt again. Afraid of getting someone else hurt. Afraid of what will happen if I let my guard down again. I don't know what to do anymore. I could really use your guidance. What should I do?"

A voice then rang out from behind him. "Well, I can tell you what you shouldn't do."

Jacobs spun around, landing on his back, reaching down for his gun. Before he pulled it out, though, he got a good look at the man's face. He took a deep breath, then got back to his feet, brushing the dirt off him.

"What are you doing here?"

Buchanan shrugged. "Just passing through."

Jacobs laughed. "Yeah, likely story. Just happened to be passing through. The first time I've been here in two months, and you're just passing through at that moment?"

Buchanan grinned. "I guess I've got good timing, huh?"

"Yeah. So how much of that did you hear?"

"Oh, not much. Just that last part, really. This is your own time, and I don't like to intrude on it."

"But you will anyway."

Buchanan shrugged again. "So what's this about letting your guard down?"

"Thought you weren't listening?"

"Just to that last part. Honestly, I thought you'd have heard me walk up on you long before I got here. I was surprised you didn't. Guess you were too deep in thought."

"Yeah."

"So what do you need guidance for? Maybe I can help."

"I'll, uh, I'll keep that to myself."

"Playing it close to the vest, huh?"

"Don't I always?"

"Now you do. You weren't always like that."

Jacobs looked over at the graves. "Yeah. Things change. So do people."

Buchanan nodded. "Don't I know it? So what's up? You got a new girl or something?"

Jacobs moved his lips to smile, but it wasn't much of one. He made an attempt though. "No." He looked at the graves again. "I'm not sure if that's ever in the cards for me again."

"It should be." Buchanan tapped him on the shoulder with the back of his hand. "Don't ever be afraid to let your guard down and have your heart go pitter-patter again. Trust me. Love can do a lot for a person. Don't ever reject it if it's there."

"Who said anything about love?"

"Well, I'm just saying. If you ever get a chance to love someone again, or have someone love you the way Val did, you jump on that. You'd be a fool to pass it up. And if there's one thing I know you're not... it's a fool."

"That's for the advice, Dr. Phil."

Buchanan laughed. "Hey, maybe I should start my own TV show, what do you think?"

Jacobs finally let out a smile. "I think the ratings would be terrible."

Buchanan continued laughing. "Yeah, you're probably right. I probably give terrible advice, anyway."

"Not always."

"So you do listen sometimes."

"Sometimes." Jacobs took the envelope out of his pocket. "This wasn't you, was it?"

Buchanan looked down at it. "No, what's that?"

Jacobs took the paper out of the envelope and showed it to him. "I dunno. Found it here, taped to Val's grave. Thought maybe it was you wanting to get in touch or something."

"You know that's not my number. And I have yours anyway. I wouldn't need to resort to these kinds of games."

"Yeah, I thought not." Jacobs put it back in his pocket. "Thought I'd check anyway, just to be sure."

Now it was Buchanan's turn to look around. "You need to be careful with that. Other people know you're here too."

"Yeah, I know. This is where they're buried though. Can't change that. And I won't stop visiting."

"Well, you could move them."

"What would be the point? Moving graves isn't exactly a clandestine operation. If they found them here, they can find them somewhere else too."

"Yeah, probably."

"So you got a man stationed here or something?" Jacobs asked.

"You really think the department could afford putting a car here indefinitely just in the hopes that you show up at some point? I told you, just happened to be passing through. Besides, even if there was a car here, we both know you'd lose them within five minutes of leaving here anyway, so what would be the point?"

Jacobs smiled. Buchanan was right on the money. But it still didn't tell him why the sergeant was there. "So what are you doing here?"

"Just wanted to talk to you about something."

"Thought we already were."

"I mean something else. It's about that schoolteacher you were seeing."

"I wasn't seeing her."

"Well, you asked me to keep tabs on if I heard anything out there, especially after that apartment incident."

"Thanks for keeping that on the down-low, by the way."

"Don't mention it. There were enough bodies there, not to mention half the place collapsing, that nobody even gave it much thought other than a gang fight between two groups. Nobody even suspected you being there."

"I still appreciate it. Anyway, what about her?"

"Word on the street is that Ames still has it out for her."

Jacobs sighed. He knew she wasn't safe yet. "Why?"

"Don't know. Can't even say a hundred percent it's her, either. No names were thrown about. It was just that Ames was looking for some girl that was connected to you. That's all there was. Doesn't take a genius to put two and two together, though. Who else would they be talking about?"

"No, it's her." Jacobs sighed again. "It's..." He shook his head. "It's just never gonna be over."

"It can be. You don't have to engage. You can walk away, you know."

"Can I?"

"Yes. You can. If you want to."

Jacobs was already starting to get tired of hearing that. It seemed that everyone kept telling him the same thing. The voices changed, sometimes the words were different, but it was the same message. Every time.

"I don't think I can. Maybe I've never really gotten the cop out of me. I see bad people out there, and I just wanna do everything in my power to get rid of them, you know?"

"Yeah. I know. That's what drove you to become a great cop. But, Brett, you're not a cop anymore. Let us handle it."

"I think it's too late for that now, isn't it?"

"No, it's not. It's never too late. Remember how we got rid of Alexander? We can do the same thing for Ames."

"Alexander was different. He wasn't connected the same way. He didn't wield the same power. Ames... he's more like Mallette. More than we know. And his power's growing, and it's gonna continue to grow if we don't put a stop to him soon."

"So let's do that."

Jacobs shook his head. "I think he's a guy that needs to be stopped permanently. You guys won't do that."

"Remember what I told you before, about climbing out of that hole? You can climb out of it now."

"If I'm out there, and Ames is out there, you really think he's gonna stop looking for me? Or Tiffany?"

"Depends on how close you are."

Jacobs looked away and shook his head again. "I'm not really interested in leaving anytime soon. I'm not gonna be run out of this city."

"No one's talking about running you out."

"Why should I be the one to leave? This guy's doing all this stuff, and yet people keep telling me I should go? What about him?"

"He'll get dealt with."

"Yeah, he will. By me."

"Now don't go talking like that," Buchanan said. "Talking like that will get you in a heap of trouble."

"We both know the law only works with what you can prove."

"Brett..."

"I'm just saying."

"I know what you're saying. And I'm saying to knock off that kind of talk."

Jacobs glared at him and nodded, though his mind wasn't changed. They continued talking for a few more minutes before Buchanan finally left. Jacobs watched as his friend walked back to his car. The words of warning had appeared to fall on deaf ears, though.

"He'll get dealt with."

4

———

J acobs was still sitting in his car. He looked out at the graves again, not yet ready to leave. He then took out the envelope again and opened it. He pulled the piece of paper out and looked at the number. He debated for a few seconds what he wanted to do. Part of him wanted to just throw the thing out the window, but the other part of him was curious about who this was and what they wanted.

Before deciding to call, though, Jacobs had to run through the list of possibilities in his mind. The likeliest person was Ames. The least likely was someone he'd never even heard of. He actually was hoping it was Ames. He wanted to talk to him again and let him know he was coming for him.

Jacobs pulled his phone out of his pocket and put his fingers on the screen, ready to dial. He punched in the numbers, then sat there and stared at it before he hit the call button. After a few seconds, he finally hit the green button. The phone rang three times before someone answered.

"I was wondering when this call would happen. I put that note there over a week ago."

It was the voice of a man Jacobs already knew. And his wish had been granted. "What do you want?"

"Not visiting the family as much as you used to?"

"I assume you have something you want to say?"

"You are perceptive, aren't you?"

"Get on with it, Ames, or else I can end this call just as fast as I started it."

"It's been a couple of months since our last encounter."

"I don't need a history lesson."

"Since I haven't seen your name pop up in any obituaries, I knew you were still alive."

"Hope that didn't disappoint you too much."

Ames laughed. "You and I have some unfinished business."

"We sure do. Only the next time we meet, I'll make sure it's finished."

"Always confident, aren't you?"

"I know what I can do. And I know what you can do. And I know you're not good enough to take me out. If you were, I wouldn't still be here."

"How's the schoolteacher holding up these days?"

"Just fine."

"How long do you think you can protect her?"

"Listen, jerk off, leave her out of this. This is now between us. Why do you need to bring her into it?"

"You're the one who brought her into it. Not me."

Jacobs sighed. He was getting angry at this pointless conversation. "Listen, if you wanna settle this once and for all, just give me a time and a place. I'll be there. Then we'll see which one of us comes out."

Ames laughed. "Yeah, you'd like that, wouldn't you? Anyway, how long do you think you can play bodyguard?"

"As long as I need to. Or whenever I kill you."

"One day, you won't be there."

"I'll be there every day if I have to. You're not stupid enough to try to do something at her school with the cameras they have around. That'd bring down more heat from the police than you're prepared to handle."

"You think you have it all figured out, but you'll slip-up one day."

"Not likely. But besides having this delightful conversation, is there anything you actually wanted, besides giving me more reason to blow your head off?"

"Actually, there is."

"Then get on with it."

"Don't ask me why, but I'm offering you a lifeline."

"Generous of you."

"Yes, and though you're not deserving of one, I feel... I don't know, well, generous. I will give you an out."

"What?"

"Yes, I will let you and your girlfriend off the hook. Leave this city within the next two weeks, and I'll take the kill order off of you. And her."

"First of all, she's not my girlfriend. She's just someone unlucky enough to stumble into this thing. Second of all, I'm not going anywhere. So you'll forgive me if I reject your offer. The only thing I really wish is that you were here to give it to me in person, that way I could shove it right up your ass."

"And what makes you think I'm not?"

"Because you're not stupid. Everyone knows I come here. You also wouldn't be the first person to try something here. You're also not dumb enough to think I come here without some kind of backup."

"If you're referring to Franks, that's not much of a backup."

"I'm not. And by the way, you can tell whatever team you got here trying to tail me to back off now and save us both the time it'll take me to lose them."

"I don't have anyone there."

Jacobs laughed. "Yeah, OK. And you think I'm just gonna go straight home and then wind up with a knock on my door in an hour?"

"I am trying to be hospitable and save your life, though I don't know why I should. If you get out of town, we both can get on with our other business."

"Right now, the only business I got is you. I didn't get a chance to kill Mallette, and Alexander I helped send to jail, but you... you're a different story. I'm anxiously looking forward to getting rid of you."

"And yet I haven't heard a thing from you in the last two months, other than seeing you take Ms. Teacher to work every day."

"I've got my own reasons for that. But don't worry, you'll be seeing me soon."

"Some people are too thick-headed to know what's good for them."

"I agree. You are. Is that what this thing was about? Giving me the opportunity to leave town in one piece?"

"Yes. I had hoped we would finally be able to come to an understanding. I can see now that that's not possible," Ames said.

"The only thing we'll come to an understanding about is me blowing your head off. You can't stop me. If you could, you wouldn't bother having this conversation. We both know your days are numbered. And those days are coming soon."

Jacobs quickly ended the conversation, wanting to leave Ames with those parting words. Still a little steamed, Jacobs shook his head and looked out his window. He couldn't believe that Ames actually thought this would work. He couldn't have possibly believed that Jacobs would just pack up and leave. As the anger started to leave his system, and Jacobs started thinking more clearly, he knew there had to be another reason for the call. There had to be something else that Ames had in mind. Jacobs just didn't know what it was. Yet.

Suddenly, Jacobs heard the sound of tires squealing. Within moments, there was another car that quickly pulled up next to him on the driver's side. Jacobs looked over and saw the barrel of a gun pointing through the open window at him. He immediately ducked and lunged himself across the passenger seat as the bullets started flying.

As his window smashed to pieces, Jacobs crawled along the seats and put his fingers on the handle of the door, opening it as fast as he could. He slid out of the car and onto the ground as his car got sprayed with bullets. He landed hard on the pavement, and on his injured shoulder. He winced for a second, but quickly shrugged off the pain as he reached for his gun in the back of his pants.

Jacobs raised his head up slightly, pointing his gun at the other car. He was just about to fire when the car sped off. Jacobs got to his feet and was about to start firing, but then thought better of it. The car was moving too fast, and he didn't want to possibly hit any cars or people that might suddenly cross into his sights. He took another look around to make sure there wasn't a second car waiting in the weeds. There was nothing that he noticed, though.

Jacobs looked at his car and shook his head at all the bullet holes now in it. "Well, I guess I know what that was about now."

He thought about getting in to see if it was still in drivable condition, though he didn't know if there was even a point to that. Having a car full of bullet holes in it stuck out like a sore thumb. All he needed was someone to drive by his place and notice a bullet-ridden car sitting there and now know where he was living. It was probably better to just ditch it altogether. Jacobs sighed and got out his phone again, this time calling Franks.

"Hey, can you come get me?"

"What?" Franks asked, somewhat alarmed at the question. "What's the matter?"

"Uh, I had a little bit of a car problem."

"What, it ain't starting?"

"Can you just come get me?"

"What about Tiff?"

"Just leave her there with Gunner."

"Uh, I don't know if that's such a good idea, man. I mean, if I leave her here alone, I don't know if it's a guarantee that she'll still be here when we get back, if you know what I mean."

"I thought you talked to her and she said it was good."

"That's now, man. But what if she's here by herself and gets those ideas in her head again and decides to take off, and there's nobody here to change her mind?"

"Uh, well, then I guess bring her. I mean, I guess ask her. We can't force her. She's not a prisoner."

"All right, fine. Where you at?"

"At the cemetery."

"OK. Everything good there?"

Jacobs looked at his car again. "Uh, yeah, every-thing's fine."

"All right. Be there in twenty."

Jacobs put his phone back in his pocket and looked around again. Everything seemed clear at the moment. But he also wasn't going to just stand there and be a target if there was a second round coming. He opened the trunk and took out his bag, which was the only thing in the car, and walked over to the side of the property. There was a fence that separated the ceme-tery grounds from the business next to it.

It was a shady spot with a bunch of trees around it, and nobody would be able to sneak up behind Jacobs, so he sat down and waited. If there was a second car that tried to finish what the other one started, he'd be able to see them coming before they got to him.

Luckily, it was a quiet twenty minutes. Jacobs really didn't want to engage in a gun battle there. Not only was it a cemetery, which was supposed to be a quiet place meant for reflection and remembrance, it was also where his family was. It didn't seem right to do that type of stuff there.

When Jacobs saw Franks' car pulling up, he grabbed his bag and stood up. The car pulled up along the curb and Jacobs walked over to it. Franks and Tiffany both got out.

"What the hell is this?!" Franks asked, pointing at Jacobs' car.

Jacobs replied calmly as if he didn't know what Franks was talking about. "What?"

"Uh, that!" Franks demonstratively moved his arms around, still pointing at Jacobs' car. "There's bullet holes in it, man."

"So? I told you I had car trouble."

Franks' face looked stunned. "Uh, yeah, you said car trouble. You didn't say it was *car trouble*!"

"Well, what's the difference?"

"The difference is someone was shooting at you, man!"

"It's fine."

Franks looked at Tiffany. "I dunno. Maybe you can talk some sense into him."

"How can you be so calm after someone shot at you?" Tiffany asked.

"Because getting worked up about it doesn't do anyone any good. Besides, they missed."

Franks looked at the car again. "They did? Looks like they had good aim to me!"

"They were aiming for me."

Franks rubbed the top of his head. "And do you happen to know who's responsible for this little situation?"

"Sure I do. It was Ames."

Franks tilted his head back and looked up at the

sky. "Oh, of course it was. Of course it was. Oh, man. What are we gonna do here?"

"Well, you could give me a lift back home for one."

"I don't mean that! I mean about this."

"I'm gonna need a new car."

"Obviously."

"Nothing's changed."

"Of course it hasn't," Tiffany said.

Jacobs looked at Tiffany. "As long as Ames is out there, I'm a target. You're a target. The only way that changes is by stopping Ames. For good."

"And how long is that going to take?"

Jacobs walked over to her and looked her in the eyes. "I wish I could be the man you want me to be."

"You can be."

"I can't. Not yet."

"You can if you want to be."

"Maybe eventually I can. But not yet."

5

Jacobs was sitting in the dark at the kitchen table. He was replaying the events of everything in his mind. He was thinking about his family, Mallette, Ames, and all the battles that he had in between. He was thinking of what he could have done differently, if anything. Then his thoughts turned to Tiffany. It wasn't fair that she was caught up in this now, he thought. He'd give anything to get her out of it.

Suddenly, the lights came on. He looked up and saw Tiffany walk over to him. She sat down next to him. She didn't know if she should, but she saw his hand on top of the table and put hers on top of his. Jacobs didn't pull away.

"What's wrong?"

Jacobs looked at her for a second without answering. She had a caring look about her. He didn't know what it was, maybe it was the teacher in her, or maybe she was just that way naturally, but she had a way of expressing herself in such a natural way. Nothing she ever said seemed forced.

"What makes you think something's wrong?" Jacobs asked.

"You've been quiet."

"I'm always quiet."

Tiffany smiled. "Not like this. What's wrong? Is it the cemetery?" She now started rubbing his hand with her thumb.

As Jacobs stared into her eyes and looked at her face, he couldn't lie to her. She had a way of drawing it out of him without even trying very hard. "Yes."

"You don't have to keep this up."

"I do." Jacobs looked down at her hand on top of his. It felt good. It felt right. He still didn't pull away.

"Why?" she asked in a much different tone than their last discussion about it. They were both talking softly this time.

Jacobs took a gulp, not really wanting to tell her everything, but knowing that he should. It was the right thing to do. Plus, she deserved to know.

"When I was talking to Ames, he indicated that you were still a target." He could immediately see the disappointment on her face.

"Oh."

"That's why I don't want you to go. If you leave here, I can't guarantee I can protect you all the time."

Tiffany wiped a tear from her eye. "When is this gonna end?"

"Soon." Jacobs then put his other hand on top of hers so that now her hand was between both of his. "I'm sorry. I didn't want for any of this to happen."

"Brett, I swear if you're gonna apologize and blame yourself again for this, then I'm gonna smack you." She forced a laugh as she got her tears under control.

"But I—"

"No. I don't wanna hear it. It's not your fault. None of this is your fault. Stop blaming yourself for other people's actions. You didn't make any of this happen to me. It was Ames' decision, not yours."

"But—"

"No. Stop. When we met, you said it probably wasn't a good idea to get involved. I heard you and listened to what you said. But I chose to ignore you, because that was my decision. You know why? Because I liked you. I still like you. And I wouldn't trade knowing you for any of it. Do I wish things were different? Yeah. But I can't be honest and say I dislike living here with you. I actually love it. I love being close to you." She smiled. "And Gunner. I love that guy. But when we're just here, I actually kind of forget all that other stuff out there. It's like it's just us and nothing else out there even matters. I feel like we're in our own little bubble. And I wouldn't mind staying here forever, if there was a light at the end of the tunnel."

"Meaning me giving up everything?"

"Meaning you finally moving on. I mean, you've told me everything that's happened, and I get it, I do. And I don't blame you for anything you've felt, or done, or anything. It's completely understandable. And I know some of the things you've done are technically against the law, and I'm gonna completely overlook that one for a second, but I get what you're doing. You wanna take bad people off the streets so other people don't have to go through what you did. And I get it. I really do. But you can't do that forever."

They continued holding hands while Jacobs deliberated on opening up more to her. He wasn't sure he should, but opening up to her felt natural.

"You know, before I met you, and I mean, right before I met you, I wasn't planning on doing this forever."

"So what changed?" Tiffany asked, not understanding his true meaning.

"I mean... I wasn't planning on continuing all this. I planned on taking out Ames, and whoever else, and... going down with them."

"Oh my god, are you serious?"

Jacobs nodded. "Yeah. I figured if I couldn't move on, then I wouldn't. And I'd finally be with my family again."

Tiffany put her free hand on top of his, so their hands were completely touching. She gripped his tighter. "Please tell me that's not in your thought process anymore."

Jacobs looked at her and shook his head. "It's not. I thought that was what I actually wanted for a while, but then something changed."

"What? What happened to change your mind?"

"You. You walked into my life, and I thought, maybe I could change. Maybe I could go back to that man I used to be."

"And you can. You really can."

Jacobs' eyes started filling with tears, though no drops fell as he got them under control. "I knew it probably wasn't a good idea to keep you close to me, and I knew I should probably push you away, but I guess I didn't really want to. When I looked at you, I thought there was still a chance for me."

"And there is. I promise you there is. But you've got to want it. And you've got to believe it."

"But I also can't just walk away from this. Not because I love it or I have a death wish or anything. But because, if I walk away, there's always going to be a piece of me that's looking over my shoulder, wondering if he's coming. If we just left now and went somewhere else, I'm always going to wonder about coming home one day and finding you lying on the floor somewhere, because I got complacent. Because I let my guard down. I can't let that happen again."

"But didn't you say he'd let you out of the city?"

"Do you really trust and believe anything he says?"

Tiffany looked away for a second. She honestly couldn't say that she did. She was already well aware of what Ames was capable of. "There has to be another way."

"There is. I finish what I started."

"That's not the way."

"It's the only way. Men like him, Mallette, that's the only way they understand. They don't understand reason. They don't understand anything other than their own greed. Believe me, I've been dealing with this stuff for a while now. I know them."

Tiffany tightened her grip on his hands. "I don't want to lose you before I even had you."

"You really think there's hope for me?"

"Yes. If you just give yourself a chance, if you give us a chance, you can be the person that you want to be."

Jacobs batted his eyes quickly and took a deep breath. "How about I make a deal with you?"

"What kind of deal?"

"You let me finish what I started here. I'll take care of Ames. And you don't get in my way of that. And you also agree to stay here until that happens."

"And if I do?"

"Then after it's over, I'll walk away from all of this."

Tiffany's face lit up. She didn't really believe he would say it. "You really would?"

Jacobs nodded. "I really would. I'll go wherever you wanna go. Whether it's somewhere else, or stay here, whatever. I'll do whatever you want. And I'll give us a chance to work. But I can't do that if I'm looking over my shoulder, wondering if there's another shoe that's going to drop. I need to know you're completely safe and out of this."

Tiffany couldn't hide her excitement. She removed her hands from his and clapped excitedly. She then leapt off her chair and jumped onto his lap. She put her hands on each side of his face, then leaned in, their faces inches apart. Their lips were close to touching. Jacobs put his arms around her, his hands resting on her back. He didn't want to pull away anymore.

Tiffany moved in closer, putting her lips on his. Jacobs reciprocated the emotion. They enjoyed each other's affection and embrace for a while. They finally pulled their lips away from each other when they heard Gunner barking. They looked down and they both laughed, seeing him sitting there, only a few feet away, watching them.

"I'm sorry, sweety, am I taking him away from you?"

"I was going to say the same thing about you," Jacob said. "You seem to be his new favorite."

Gunner barked at them a couple more times, causing Jacobs and Tiffany to laugh some more.

"Do you think he's upset with us?" Tiffany asked.

"Are you kidding? I think he loves you more than me."

Gunner then ran out of the room and over to the window in the living room. He continued barking.

Jacobs knew something was up. Tiffany got off his lap, and the two of them went over to the window and looked out. They saw Franks approaching.

"Oh, nobody important," Jacobs said.

Tiffany playfully slapped him on the arm. "Hey, be nice. Eddie's good to you."

"You have no idea the things I've put up with over the years from him."

"I know he's a little strange at times, but he cares about you."

"I know. I just wish he wouldn't talk so much." Jacobs went over to the door and opened it as Franks got there.

"Well, well, well, it's nice to get this kind of service for once," Franks said, walking in. "If I were wearing a cape, this would be the part where I turn around for you to take it off me and hang it up."

Jacobs wore a confused face, as he often did when talking to his friend, and closed the door. "What?"

"Never mind, man, never mind. Anyways..."

"Why are you here?"

"Oh, well, that's what I was here to talk to you about."

"What?"

"Why I'm here."

"Which is?"

"I got something to tell you."

"I figured that. What?"

"What what?"

"Oh my god." Jacobs ran his hand over his head and looked at Tiffany. "You see? You see what I've been dealing with all this time?"

Tiffany laughed, thinking it was cute. She knew Jacobs wasn't really mad, he just liked to pretend that he was. It was their own bromance type of thing.

"So what is it?" Jacobs asked.

"What's what?"

"What you came over here for?"

Franks looked at the wall as if he were trying to remember. Jacobs put his head down and sighed. He shook his head, then walked over to the couch and sat down.

"Oh!" Franks shouted.

"What?"

"I remembered."

Jacobs looked up at the ceiling and grinned. He really had no other words. "Great. Would you mind telling the rest of us?"

"Oh, yeah. Of course I will. Don't be impatient."

Jacobs put his hand on his forehead, trying to remain calm. "Wouldn't dream of it."

"So I got you a new car."

"What?"

Franks slapped both his legs. "Do I stutter, man? I said I got you a new car."

"That was fast."

Franks had a pleased look on his face, and he rubbed his fingernails on his shirt as if he were polishing them. "Yeah, well, they don't call me the best for nothing."

Jacobs went over to the window and looked out. "Which one is it?"

Franks reached into his pocket and removed some keys. He then pushed a button to unlock and lock the car, the lights quickly shining on and off. "That one."

"Looks black."

"Got a problem with that?"

Jacobs smiled. "Nope."

"Good. It's pretty much the same as your last one. This one's a little newer."

"I thought you said it was new?"

"Well, it is. New to you. Not new to the world. It's been hanging around for a few years now, but it's only got about forty thousand miles on it, so it's in good condition. Plates and registration have been changed and all, so you're good to go with it."

Jacobs took the keys. "Thanks. I appreciate it."

"Anything for you, my man."

Jacobs went into the kitchen and put the keys in a drawer. As he left the room, Franks quickly rushed over to Tiffany and stood next to her.

"How's it been going? You been working him?"

Tiffany smiled. "Yeah. I've been doing my best."

"Any progress?"

"Yeah. I feel we're making some."

"Good, good. Keep at it. We'll break him down yet."

Jacobs walked back into the room. "What are you guys talking about?"

"Huh?" Franks said. "Oh, nothing, nothing. Just seeing how she was doing. Making sure you weren't boring her to death or anything."

"Really?" Jacobs walked back over to the couch and sat down.

Tiffany walked over to the couch too and sat down next to him. Jacobs suddenly put his arm around her and brought her in close to him, her head resting on his shoulder. Franks' eyes almost popped out of his head. He couldn't believe it. He took a few steps back, then started looking around.

"Uh, uh... am I in the right place?" Franks continued looking around. "I feel like I stepped into an alternate universe or something."

Tiffany laughed.

"Why?" Jacobs asked.

Franks turned his head to the side slightly, though still looking at the two of them. He pointed at them, brought his finger back in front of his face, then tucked it back into his fist. "No, I must be seeing things or something. This can't be happening. What I think is happening can't be happening." He turned away for a second, then looked back at them. "Is it?"

"Is what?"

"Is it you and... her, I mean, the two of you... are you... you know... I mean... together?"

Tiffany sat up straight, Jacobs taking his arm off her, though she put her hand on his knee. "Brett said that after Ames is done, then so is he."

A half-smile on Franks' face slowly turned into a big one. "He said what now?"

Jacobs took a deep breath. "After I take out Ames, then I'm walking away."

"You're serious?"

Jacobs nodded, then looked at Tiffany. "She sees something in me that I'm not sure is there. But I'm willing to give it a shot and hope that she's right."

"I am," Tiffany replied.

"Well, I'll be," Franks said. "I was beginning to think I'd never see the day. So what are you gonna do after Ames is gone?"

"I don't know. Let's not jump the bucket and over-look him too fast though, huh? I mean, he's not exactly a slouch."

"Yeah, you're right, you're right. But, uh, what does that mean for you?" Franks pointed at Tiffany. "Am I still looking for another place for you or what?"

Tiffany looked at Jacobs. "You already know my feelings," he said.

Tiffany smiled. "I'll stay here. As long as you promise you're done after this."

Jacobs nodded. "I am."

Tiffany looked back at Franks. "Then you can stop looking. I'm where I want to be."

Franks smiled and let out a little laugh. "Good. Gotta be honest, I wasn't really looking." He saw Tiffany shoot him a look. "I mean, I was going to and all, I mean, I was planning on getting you this real nice place, but now, guess I don't need to proceed with that. There was a chance it might fall through anyway."

Tiffany laughed as well, knowing he was talking nonsense. She didn't mind as much as Jacobs did, though. Franks, getting the sense the two of them were growing closer, and maybe wanted some time alone, started heading for the door.

"Leaving already?" Tiffany asked.

"Uh, yeah, well, I got some things to do, and I don't wanna be in the way of you two getting your spurs on and all, so I think I'm just gonna head out now. You two get on that horse now, hear?"

Tiffany looked confused as Franks led himself out the door. Once the door closed, she turned to Jacobs.

"What did all of that even mean?"

Jacobs put his hand up. "Don't even. Don't even try to comprehend anything he just said. It makes sense to him in some twisted sort of way, so just let it be and don't even try. If you try, you'll only make your head hurt."

"Oh. OK."

"You know, I don't think you ever gave me a response to my deal."

"Yes, I did."

"No, you just leapt out of your chair. You never said you agreed."

Tiffany laughed. "Well, that was my response."

"So is that a yes?"

She moved in closer, her lips right against his. "This is the only answer you need."

6

The guard led his prisoner through the door and directed him to the table. It wasn't Mallette's usual table, but then again, he hadn't had a visitor in months. Mallette eyed the man who was sitting there waiting for him. He already had some ideas in his head as to who it might be, judging by the way he dressed. Expensive-looking shoes, slicked back black hair, briefcase, and he was looking over some papers. He was either an attorney, or he was looking for information that he hoped Mallette would spill.

Neither was all that appealing to Mallette at the moment. He'd already had his fill of both kinds in the time he'd been in prison. Ever since he arrived there, he'd had lawyers telling him they were getting him out, or people from law enforcement hoping to get more information out of him in exchange for some perk. He wasn't that interested in either one anymore. Still, he was already there, so hearing the man out seemed to be the only thing to do.

Mallette sat down across from the man, not looking especially happy. The man put his papers down and looked up. He was a little intimidated by the sight of an angry face looking at him. It wasn't quite what he pictured when he walked in there. He thought Mallette would look more hopeful than he did. He put his hand out to shake, but Mallette didn't move his hands an inch. The man gulped, then brought his hand back in front of him.

"I guess you're wondering who I am and why you're here?" Mallette continued staring at him, not saying a word. "OK. Yes, well, my name is Andrew Berry." Berry had hoped that Mallette would say something at this point, but his hopes were quickly dashed. "And, uh, I am now here to represent you."

Berry looked on with a smile, thinking that would get some type of response out of Mallette. It did not. Berry looked somewhat confused and nervous, and he was unsure of what to say next.

"You do want representation, do you not?"

Mallette continued looking at the man. He seemed like the rest of the lawyers he had. Nothing different. They couldn't get him out. He saw no reason to expect anything different this time.

"I've been looking over your case, and I think there are a few things we could try to hit on to secure an early release for you."

"Do I look like an idiot," Mallette finally said.

Berry was a bit thrown off by the question. "Uh, no. Of course not."

"And you have the audacity to come in here, someone I don't even know, and you start talking like you can get me an early release."

"I, um…"

"Do you know how many times I've heard that in the last couple years? Do you know how many lawyers have sat in your seat and told me the exact same thing?"

"Uh, I am aware that you've had several lawyers before me, and while I'm not questioning their capabilities, I am quite confident I can succeed where they failed."

"And why is that?"

"Because I have more to gain than they do. In addition to getting you out, I am also proposing a deal."

"What kind of deal?"

"If I am able to secure your release, you agree to keep me on as your legal counsel indefinitely, and pay me double the going rate."

Mallette looked unmoved by his demands. "If you get me out of here, I'll pay you triple the going rate. I'll buy you a house, a car, and anything else you want. I'll keep you employed until long after your faculties have left you. Just get me out."

Berry smiled. "Well, OK then. That's good news. I think we have a deal. And I am quite confident in saying that you can start marking the days you have left in here on a calendar. Because they are numbered."

Jacobs was sitting on the back porch, not doing anything but soaking up the sun and watching Gunner frolic around. Tiffany came up behind him and put her arms around him, giving him a kiss on the cheek.

"Hey."

"What are you doing?" she asked.

Jacobs shook his head. "Nothing. Just sitting."

"Oh. Nice."

Jacobs peeked over at her as she sat down in the chair next to him. He got the feeling there was something on her mind.

"Something you wanna talk about?"

"No, nothing specific, why?"

"Just seemed like there might be something on your mind."

"No, not really."

Jacobs still thought there was, but he wasn't going to push her. He figured she'd say it when she was ready. It didn't take as long as he thought it would.

"OK, there is something I wanted to talk to you about."

Jacobs grinned. "I thought there was."

"You know, I'm not sure how you're gonna feel about this."

"About what?"

"Um..."

"Tiff, just say it. You don't need to worry about anything."

"OK. Well, I got a message from my mom yesterday."

"And?"

"Well, as you know, I haven't seen my parents in a couple of months, since all this happened."

"Yeah?"

"As you also know, I used to see them every week."

"I know."

"And they would like to meet for dinner or something. And I don't know what to tell them."

"I'm not sure that's a good idea. Ames might have someone watching them."

"That's another thing. Should I at least tell them what's going on, that way they can be prepared or at least be on the lookout for something?"

"No, don't worry them unnecessarily."

"But what if something happens to them? What if Ames starts to use them to get to me, in order to get to you?"

Jacobs stared at her for a few seconds. He hadn't really considered the possibility before, but he couldn't deny it was possible and made sense. He wouldn't put it past Ames to do that. He'd already shown he was willing and capable of doing so.

"If something happens to them..."

"Nothing's gonna happen to them," Jacobs said.

"But you can't be with me, dealing with Ames, and protecting them at the same time." Jacobs looked up at the blue sky as he thought about it. "And I also wanna see them. I mean, I've been telling them I've been so busy with work stuff, but I can't say that forever before they think I'm blowing them off or lying to them."

Jacobs looked at her briefly, still thinking. "OK. Why don't I call Eddie and ask if he knows someone who can watch your parents' place?"

Tiffany smiled. "Thank you. That would really help me sleep a lot better and not worry so much. As long as it's someone who really knows what they're doing and not sleeping on the job or something."

"I'll tell him it's gotta be somebody top-notch."

Tiffany leaned over and kissed him on the cheek again. "Thank you. What about the other thing?"

"What other thing?"

"I really wanna see them. I like being here, and spending time with you is great, but I also don't wanna be cooped up here all the time."

"They saw us at the park before."

"There are other parks. There are other things to do out there. And if we just decide to go out somewhere, they're not gonna be there waiting. We know how they found us at the park."

Jacobs ran his hand over his head. "Yeah, I know. I just like to play it extra cautious."

"I know. And I appreciate all you're doing for me. But we still have to live."

"I know." Jacobs wanted to protect her as much as possible, but he knew how important family was. He of all people knew. He couldn't deny her seeing them. If anybody knew that you couldn't just assume there would be another day to see or talk to them, it was him. "If you wanna go out and see them, that's fine."

Tiffany smiled and kissed him again. "Thank you."

"You don't have to thank me. You're not a prisoner here. You can do what you want. You don't need my permission for anything. I just wanna make sure whatever you do, you're safe."

"I know. I just know how protective you are and wanted to make sure you didn't give me a hard time about it first."

"I won't. Not when it comes to your family. Just let me know when you wanna see them."

"Maybe we could meet them for dinner this week?"

"Uh, we?"

Tiffany smirked. "Yeah. You and me. We."

"Uh, why me?"

Tiffany shrugged. "I don't know. I mean, we're living together, and it seems like things are progressing with us. I just thought it'd be a nice thing to meet my parents. And for them to meet you."

"Uh, I'm not really sure that's a good idea."

"Why not?"

"I'm not sure they're ready for me."

Tiffany laughed. "Of course they're ready for you. Why do you make it sound like you're some type of alien or something? You're perfectly normal."

"I'm not sure what I would say."

"You can say anything. They're really nice. They're not judgmental or anything like that."

"Have you actually told them anything about me?"

"Uh, well..."

"Tiff!"

"All I told them was that I met this really nice guy, and we got along really well. I said we were taking things slow, but it was going good."

"And?"

"And that's it. My mother said they'd like to meet you at some point, so I thought maybe if we met them for dinner, you could get to know them."

"And they get to know me."

"Is that so bad?"

Jacobs tilted his head and made a face. "It's just that... the last few years, I've spent a lot of time trying to make sure nobody got to know me."

"Well, if you're gonna go back to being the old you, this is a good first step, don't you think?"

Jacobs looked down, thinking of his options. There really weren't any, though. Not if he really wanted a life similar to the one he used to have. If he really did want to give his current life up, and pursue a relationship with Tiffany, he was going to have to do some things that made him uncomfortable. Some things that he never thought he'd do again. As he sat there thinking, Tiffany slipped her hand into his.

"I'll help you get through it."

Jacobs looked at her and smiled. She just had one of those faces that melted his heart. He didn't know what she saw in him, but hoped she wouldn't stop seeing whatever it was.

"If you think it's a good idea... then... OK."

Tiffany grinned. "Really? You'll do it for me?"

Jacobs nodded. "For you."

"I know you're nervous about it, but I promise everything will be fine. I wouldn't bring you into something I didn't think you could handle or were ready for."

Jacobs nodded again. "I trust you."

Tiffany put her hand on the side of his face and rubbed it. "All you have to do is be yourself. That's all. You don't have to be someone else. Just be you. And they'll see what I see."

"I should call Eddie and see if he can get to work on getting someone at your parents' place." Jacobs pulled out his phone and dialed his friend's number. Franks picked up immediately, answering enthusiastically.

"Heyooo."

Jacobs pulled the phone away from his ear for a second, putting it back to his ear when he thought Franks was done. "Can't you just say hello normally?"

Franks laughed. "Well, you know, just thought it'd give it some extra pizzazz."

"Oh. Well, mission accomplished then, I guess."

"Thanks. So what's on the old chuck wagon board tonight?"

"What?"

"What are you calling for?"

Jacobs shook his head, ignoring his previous question. "Um, I just wanted to see if you knew anyone who could sit on Tiffany's parents' place?"

"Why, you heard something? They in trouble?"

"No, not yet. And nothing that I know of. I just wanna be proactive in this case. Ames has shown he's willing to include outside people in this. If he can't get to Tiffany, who's to say he wouldn't try them?"

"Well, yeah, you got a point there. I wouldn't put nothing past that man. Nothing. With a capital N-O."

"I can't sit on them myself, so I was wondering if you knew anyone who could do the job?"

"Uh, yeah, let me think on it a bit. But I think I might have a few candidates that can do the job."

"They gotta be good, Eddie. They gotta be good. And they gotta be reliable."

"What, you think I'm just gonna send over any old slob over there? I know how important this is. Trust me. Let me do my thing."

"OK. Do your thing. They just better be good. As good as if I were doing it myself."

"Yeah, yeah, I hear ya. I'm thinking. Yeah, I think I might have someone."

"Are they good?"

"Don't even ask that question again, man. Don't even ask. I got this. You and the new missus need this, I got it. Don't you worry about it."

"Me and the who?"

Franks laughed. "OK, so it might be a bit presumptuous of me on that last part, you know what I mean? But, you know, just some wishful thinking there, you know?"

"Yeah, sure. Just try to get on this as soon as you can."

"I'll do what I can. What about payment, though? If I get someone good, it's gonna cost you."

"A thousand a day for as long as it's needed."

"What if this goes on for months?"

"For as long as it's needed."

"OK, OK, I got ya. But I also know you're not swimming in money. I know you're not hurting either, but, uh, where you gonna get the bread to pay for all this?"

"I'll worry about that. I still have a bunch saved up from some of my former raids. I can swing it for a while before I need to come up with more."

"All right, all right, as long as you're good."

"I'm good. You just do your part and get me someone."

Franks laughed. "Don't you worry. I know a guy."

7

Jacobs and Tiffany had just left the restaurant after eating dinner with her parents. It didn't go as badly as Jacobs had feared. Actually, it went pretty well. After his initial nervousness, he seemed to have a pretty good time. They all seemed to get along; there was a good bit of laughing going on, and they seemed to genuinely like him. At least as much as someone could after an initial encounter.

They stood outside the building, waiting to leave until Tiffany's parents got in their car and drove away first. Jacobs took a quick look around, seeing a man in a car a few spots down from her parents. The man locked eyes with Jacobs, then they both gave a slight nod to each other. It was the bodyguard. Jacobs had met him a few days earlier and gave him his seal of approval.

Franks picked a winner as far as Jacobs was

concerned. The man's name was Nathan Thrower. An apt name for a bodyguard, Jacobs thought. Thrower was an ex-Navy SEAL who now hired himself out to people who needed protective services. Thrower didn't just sell himself out to the highest bidder, though. He considered each case carefully, and if he didn't believe in the cause of the person hiring him, he had no problem walking away. Mostly, Thrower didn't protect bad guys and criminals from other bad guys and criminals. He also didn't protect them from law enforcement or anyone else who might have been looking for them.

But if there was an innocent person who needed help, even if they didn't have the money to pay him, Thrower wasn't one to look the other way. Before following Tiffany's parents, Thrower gave Jacobs the thumbs-up sign, letting him know they weren't followed to the restaurant. That put Jacobs' mind at ease a little bit, knowing he wouldn't have to drive around aimlessly for half an hour to get home.

Tiffany's parents pulled out of the parking lot with Thrower right behind them. Jacobs and Tiffany stood there for a few seconds, Jacobs watching carefully to make sure nobody else followed them out. Tiffany had been hanging out with Jacobs long enough to know when something didn't seem right to her.

She tugged on Jacobs' arm. "Brett, did you see that one car leave right after my parents?"

Jacobs already knew what she was getting at. "It's the guy I hired to look after them."

Tiffany let out a deep breath. "Oh, thank god. I thought…"

Jacobs smiled. "I know. But it's fine. They're in good hands. Eddie picked a good one."

"Did you meet him?"

"Yeah, I met him the other day. Solid guy. Ex-SEAL. He knows his stuff. He'll protect your parents. I have no doubt about that."

"At least that's somewhat of a relief."

"I won't let anything happen to them. I promised you."

She grinned. "I know. Thank you." She reached up and gave him a kiss. "Speaking of my parents, everything went pretty good in there, right?"

It was hard for Jacobs to admit it. "Yeah, I guess it went OK."

"OK? It went more than OK. Admit it, you had a good time."

Jacobs finally smiled. "It was… not bad."

"That's all you're gonna give me, huh?"

"Well, they seemed to not hate me."

"Oh, stop. They really liked you."

"For now."

"For always. Stop doing that."

"What?"

"Doubting yourself. There's nothing wrong with you."

"I'm just… I'm not sure I'm any parents' dream of what they want for their daughter when they dream it up."

"All they want is my happiness. And if you treat me well, and I'm happy, then they're happy. I think that's all that any parent wants for their child."

Jacobs had a hard time wiping the smile off his face as he looked at her. "Maybe."

"C'mon, let's go back to the house and check in on the baby."

Jacobs' eyes widened. "Baby?"

"Our fur-baby."

Jacobs wiped his forehead. "Oh."

Tiffany laughed. "That's my baby!"

"I know quite a few gentlemen with teeth marks in their arms who may not agree with you on that one."

"Well, they just don't know him like I do."

"I'm thankful for that."

Thrower pulled onto the Vogel's street, parking several houses down from theirs. The Vogels lived in a nice development, each house having about a quarter of an acre of property. And all the houses were two floors and around two thousand square feet. Thrower's position gave him a clear view of the house.

For most people, sitting there for long periods of time with nothing to do but stare and wait would have been boring. And to some degree it was. But for Thrower, he always kept alert. He felt that the moment he let his guard down, the second he looked away, the five minutes he closed his eyes, that's when something bad would happen to the people he was trying to protect. And that was how he was always able to keep focus. If he slacked off, someone might get killed. And he wasn't having that. Not on his watch.

Thrower sat there, watching the Vogels get out of the car and walk into their house. As boring as it was just sitting there, he didn't yearn for any action either. If there was action, that meant someone was getting hurt. Probably somebody else, but still, he didn't enjoy beating people up, or the occasional jobs where he had to do worse bodily harm to someone. He was good at it, but he preferred the downtime.

Unfortunately, this was not going to be one of those boring nights. Almost immediately after the Vogels stepped inside their home, another car slowly rolled onto the street. Thrower's eyes immediately went to the car. It was only going ten miles per hour. Thrower had a bad feeling about it. Being at this job for a couple years now, he had a sense about when things were about to go bad. And he was getting that sense now.

The car finally came to a stop in front of the Vogels' neighbor's house. From his vantage point, Thrower could see two men in the car, both in the front seats. He didn't take his eyes off the car. But he made sure he was ready to move at a moment's notice.

The men stayed in the car for a good five minutes. Thrower wasn't sure what they were waiting for.

Maybe it was just to make sure the Vogels were home. Thrower's eyes glanced at the house, seeing a few lights turn on and off. There was no question if the men were there for the Vogels; they knew they were now home.

Then Thrower noticed the driver's side door open. As the driver got it, then the passenger door opened. Both men stood near their doors and looked around. Thrower had seen that look before. They were checking to see if they were being watched by any neighbors. If they were, they'd probably stall or get back in their car, or walk around, something to make it seem like they were doing anything but what they were there for. Thrower opened his door slightly, ready to jump out depending on what the men did.

The two men approached the Vogels' house, though they veered off to the side. They were walking to the side gate that led into the backyard. The Vogels had one of those white vinyl fences surrounding their yard, and there were a good deal of trees on the perimeter, so the men were liking that they'd probably be concealed for the most part.

Thrower waited until the men were out of sight, allowing him to approach without them seeing him. He ran over to the house, stopping at the corner and peeking around. The side gate was closed now. Thrower took a few steps and slowly undid the lever, pulling the gate open. He was ready for a fight, but there was no one there. The men must've already been at the back door.

Thrower quickly rushed to the corner of the house and peeked around. There they were. It looked like they were just about ready to break through the door. Thrower walked out from the corner of the house, making himself plainly visible. He loudly cleared his throat to make himself known.

"Do you guys really think you should be doing that?"

The two men jumped back. "Who the hell are you?" one of them said.

"Oh, I just happened to be walking by, saw you two come back here."

"Well, we live here, OK?"

"Uh, pretty sure you don't. See, I know the people who live here, and you two don't look anything like them."

"Listen, guy, beat it before something bad happens to you."

"Look, people make mistakes, I get it. But if you wanna correct this one before you both wind up unconscious, I'd suggest taking a hike right now."

"Is he messing with us?" the man said to his partner. He then laughed. "Does he really think he could take on the both of us?" the man turned his attention back to Thrower. "Is that what you're implying? You think you could take both of us out at the same time?"

Thrower shrugged. He didn't look concerned. "If you really wanna find out."

The man laughed again, glancing at his partner. "You know, it never fails. You run into these cocky pricks all the time. Think they're big and tough and bad, and they talk a good game, then they get into a real fight, and they fold like Jell-O."

"Listen, guys, why don't you do yourselves a favor and get out of here, huh?"

"No. I don't think we will."

"You wanna do it the hard way, huh?"

The two men walked over to Thrower, standing only inches away from him. Thrower wasn't the least bit intimidated, even though he was outnumbered. He was quite confident in his abilities, even against two men. Thrower glanced at each of them, waiting for one of them to make the first move, and he knew it was coming.

Then, the talker of the pair threw a left hook at Thrower's face. Thrower quickly dodged it by ducking, then threw a left hand of his own at the man, which connected. Thrower instantly got hit with a punch from the other man, making him shuffle his feet, but he quickly returned the shot with one of his own. The other man got back in the fight, giving Thrower quite a workout trying to fend off two men.

Luckily for Thrower, they weren't the most skilled combatants he'd ever come up against. They were decent, but they were hardly anyone's definition of people to be scared of. The three continued fighting in the backyard over the next several minutes, all the men getting in their fair share of punches. At no point in time did Thrower ever feel like he was losing the battle, though.

The only thing the other men had going for them was the fact that there were two of them. If it was a one-on-one fight, Thrower would have dispatched both of them quite easily by now. But the two of them together were giving him a bit of a workout. But he never felt overmatched. It just would take a little longer to get rid of the both of them.

Finally, after a few more minutes, Thrower started wearing them down. He was able to get a little space between them, and started using some of his jiu-jitsu moves. A few kicks to the legs, a few kicks to the stomach, and then, finally, a few kicks to the head, and both men wound up down for the count for good.

As Thrower stood over the two men, he heard a noise by the house. It was the back door opening. Mr. Vogel stood there, looking shocked at what was going on.

"What are you guys doing on my property?"

Thrower took a few deep breaths and put his hand up. "Don't worry, sir. I've got it under control."

"Who are you guys? What are you doing here?"

"I'm an undercover detective, sir. Happened to be driving by and saw these guys poking around your fence here. So I came over to investigate."

"You're a cop?"

Thrower nodded. "That's right. Don't worry. It's all over now. You can go back inside now if you will, so I can escort these two back to jail."

"Oh. Will you need me for anything?" Mr. Vogel asked.

"No. Nothing to worry about on your end. Since I witnessed everything, you're not needed. It's all good. Thank you."

"Uh, well, thank you."

"My pleasure, sir. Have a good night."

Mr. Vogel went back inside, though he went over to a window so he could still see what was happening. Thrower looked down at the two men, who were both clearly still out of the fight. They weren't knocked out, but they weren't going to be any more of a problem. Thrower needed a few more seconds before he got his breathing normal again after the exertion. Now he had to figure out what he was going to do with the pair.

Thrower looked out the side gate and did the only thing he could think of. He'd have to neutralize the pair permanently. He picked the one man up, then to make sure he truly wasn't going to give him more of a problem, he reared back and delivered a powerful shot right to the man's nose.

The man instantly cried out and held his nose. "Ow, man, I think you broke it."

Thrower hoisted the man over his shoulder and then carried him out of the yard. He went through the gate and walked back to the car the men arrived in. He then released his grip of the man once he got next to the car, letting him fall hard on his shoulder in the grass.

"Ow! What are you trying to do?"

"Shut up or I'll break every bone in your body," Thrower said.

He opened the driver's side door and then pulled the lever by the seat to release the trunk. Once it opened, Thrower picked the man up again and shoved him into the trunk. He closed it and walked back into the yard.

Once he got there, he saw the man slowly getting back to his feet. Seeing Thrower approach, the man tried his luck one more time. He tried throwing a punch, which Thrower easily ducked.

"Didn't you learn your lesson the first time?" Thrower asked.

He then countered the man's punch by delivering a spinning kick to the man's midsection. With the man hunched over, Thrower lifted his leg up high, then let it come down hard on the back of the man's neck and head, sending him straight down to the ground. Thrower then grabbed the man from behind and started dragging him out of the yard. He dragged him all the way beside the car. He let go of him so he could open the trunk again.

As Thrower turned around, the man quickly got to

his feet again and tried his luck for a third time. He tried throwing a punch that Thrower blocked.

"Some people just don't get it, do they?"

Thrower then delivered a short, left jab to the man's face, stunning him for a moment. Thrower then grabbed him by the back of the head and rammed his face into the side of the car. The man dropped to the ground, screaming in agony and holding his head. Thrower picked him up and shoved him in the trunk with his partner.

Not wanting to stand there for too long with a couple of people in the trunk, Thrower looked around. He didn't see anyone watching, but he was still uncomfortable. He got in the car, seeing that the keys were left in the ignition. He then drove off the street, but stayed in the same development, parking on the next street over. He got out of the car and walked back to the trunk. He tapped on it a few times.

"Hey, you guys stay nice and still back there, and I'll let you out soon."

He really had no intention of letting them out anytime soon, but he just wanted to make sure they didn't make a lot of noise and bring attention to the car. If they did, Thrower would just move it again. But now that the imminent danger was over, Thrower had to get rid of his cargo. He pulled out his phone and called Jacobs.

"Hey, how's it going?" Jacobs asked. "Everything all right?"

"Well, had a little bit of a problem here."

"What happened? They try something?"

"Tried, yeah. Don't worry. I got it all under control."

"What happened?"

"As soon as the Vogels got home, another car pulled up. Two men got out, went into the back and were about to break in through the back door."

"You stopped them?"

"Yeah, they're neutralized," Thrower replied.

"What'd you do with them?"

"Well, right now they're in the trunk of their car. I got it on the next street over."

"They dead?"

Thrower laughed. "No, but I doubt they'll be fighting anyone else for a while. I gave it to them pretty good. I don't know what you want me to do with them, though. Want me to take them somewhere? Leave them? What?"

"No, I'd rather you sit on the house. Probably won't have any other action tonight, but just to be sure."

"I agree."

"Leaving them there probably isn't the best bet, either."

"What, then?"

Jacobs thought of what he could do with them. And he had a plan. "Just sit tight. I'll come and get them."

"What are you gonna do with them?"

"Send a message."

8

J acobs immediately called Franks to come give
him a lift to Thrower's position. He left Tiffany
and Gunner at home. Once they pulled up to the
car, they saw Thrower leaning up against the hood.
Jacobs went over to him, and they shook hands.

"Hey, thanks. Appreciate you doing a good job."

Thrower shrugged. Though he didn't need compli-
ments to do a good job, it was still nice to hear. "That's
what I get paid for, right?"

"In the trunk still?"

"Yep." Thrower smiled. "All nice and quiet."

"Good." Jacobs then got in the front seat of the car.
"Eddie, you follow me."

"Right behind you, man," Franks replied.

"Where you taking them?" Thrower asked.

"I'm gonna drop them right on Ames' lap," Jacobs
answered. "You need me to take you back to your car?"

Thrower shook his head. "No, it's cool. It's just the next street over. I can walk."

"All right. I'm sure the rest of your night will be uneventful, but if it's not, you got my number."

Thrower nodded. "You got it, man."

Thrower stepped away from the car and started walking away. Jacobs put the car in drive with Franks following right behind him. They drove for about twenty minutes, and though even Franks didn't know where they were going, he was sure Jacobs had something big in mind.

They arrived on the outskirts of a building, probably a warehouse or a storage building. Jacobs had been there before. He'd seen Ames' men operating out of here. There was a metal gate that was closed, but there was only a padlock and chain keeping it that way. That wasn't going to deter Jacobs. He put the car in drive and raced for the gate, busting it completely open. Franks followed him through it, stopping once they got to the main building, which wasn't far away from the gate. Both men got out of their respective cars at the same time.

"Man, that was something," Franks said. "You do that often?"

"No. I wasn't even sure it would work."

"Well, it looked pretty cool from where I was sitting."

"Now we go to the plan."

"Before we get to all that, man, I'd like an apology from you."

Jacobs looked confused. "For what?"

"For doubting me."

"Huh? What are you talking about?"

"Thrower. Admit it, you had some doubts about me finding someone capable, didn't you?"

Jacobs rolled his eyes. "Are we really gonna do this now?"

"Why not? There's nobody else here but us chickens. Admit it, you didn't think I could pull it off, did you?"

"OK, I admit. At first, I questioned whether you could find someone good enough for the job. OK? Is that what you wanna hear?"

"Yes."

"Good. Can we move on now?"

"Yeah, he's pretty good, isn't he? I mean, he took on them two dudes by himself. That's no small feat, you know," Franks said.

"I'm aware. Can we move on?"

"I mean, one's pretty good, but two's even better."

"So you've mentioned. Can we..."

"I wish I was there to see it. To see how he took down them two guys..."

"Eddie... focus."

"I am focusing."

"I mean on what we're doing here. Now."

"Oh. Guess I got a little carried away there, huh?"

"No more than usual."

"Speaking of that, what do you got cooking up your sleeve here? You never did tell me what you were planning."

"I'm gonna call the number that was left for me back at the cemetery," Jacobs said.

"And do what?"

"I'm gonna tell him I've got a present for him here."

"What if he don't pick up? What if this number is out of service? What if it was only a one time thing? What if..."

"Eddie, just let me call and find out."

"Oh. Yeah, all right, man. Go ahead."

Jacobs pulled out his phone and scrolled to the number he knew belonged to Ames. He didn't have expectations one way or another. He hoped someone would answer, but if not, he'd gift wrap the men inside the car in some other way. As soon as he dialed, he heard it ringing. He looked at Franks and nodded, letting him know it still seemed to be good.

Finally, a man answered. It wasn't Ames, though. "Yeah?"

"I wanna talk to Ames."

"Who's this?"

"Brett Jacobs."

"You wanna leave a message?"

"No. What I got to say I wanna say directly to him."

"Well, he's busy at the moment."

"Un-busy him or else he's gonna be short a few more men."

The man didn't reply at first. It took him a few seconds to think about it. "Hold on."

Jacobs leaned up against the car as he patiently waited for Ames to get on the line. It took about two minutes, but eventually the boss got on the phone.

"I can't say this was entirely expected," Ames said.

"Yeah, well, I guess I can be full of surprises too, huh?"

"So what do I owe the pleasure of hearing your voice again?"

"Tiffany's parents are off limits."

Ames decided to take the play-stupid approach. "I don't know what you're talking about."

"Oh yes, you do. Two men were sent to the Vogel's house tonight."

"News to me."

"No, it's not. They're your men. You're the one who sent them."

"And you're telling me all this because?"

"Just to let you know your plan didn't work. What? You thought I wouldn't think you'd stoop so low? That I wouldn't be prepared for it? I've got a newsflash for you: I'm already ahead of you. And you can't use them to get to me either."

"Well, I'm glad you've got it all figured out then."

"I've also got a present for you."

"You shouldn't have."

"You're right, I shouldn't. But I did. Come to 1847 Westview Drive."

"Sounds like a familiar place."

"It should. It's yours."

"And what will I find once I get there?"

Jacobs didn't reply and hung up.

"So what's the scoop?" Franks asked.

Jacobs shrugged. "I dunno. I guess he's coming."

"You didn't get a confirmation?"

"I said what I wanted to say. The rest is up to him."

"So what exactly is your plan here, anyway? You gonna gun them all down once they get here?"

Jacobs looked disappointed. "No, I don't think I'm equipped for that. Also depends on how many men he brings, or whether he actually comes himself."

"So what are we doing? Just dropping the car and leaving?"

"No. We're gonna watch and see."

Franks looked around, not seeing any good spots. "Watch from where?"

Jacobs pointed over Franks' left shoulder. "Right over there. There's a group of trees and bushes right in front of the fence. We could blend in nicely right there."

Franks looked at his car. "Uh, that's kinda gonna stick out like a sore thumb."

"Well, you obviously would have to move it."

"I got a better idea."

"Which is?"

"How about you go over in those bushes, and I'll sit in the car down the street, that way if you gotta jet out of here in a hurry or something, I can swoop the car in, you can hop through the window, and I can wing us off to safety? What do you think of that?"

"What? Afraid of something?"

"No, man, of course not. You know me. I am the bastion of courage."

"You are, huh?"

"Of course. Have you ever known me to run from a fight?"

"We don't have that much time to list it."

"Please. Haven't I run into the fire enough times to save your hide to get a... a..."

"A what?"

"I dunno. I forgot where I was going with that."

"Whatever. If you wanna go sit in the car down the street, that's fine."

"Cool. I'll make sure I still got a view of the front wherever I go. If you get in trouble, you call me on the old Batphone."

Jacobs nodded and reached into the car for his weapon. As he went over to the bushes, Franks took the car and peeled out of the property. Jacobs didn't know how long it would take for Ames to get there, but he assumed it wouldn't be a long wait. And he was right. He only had to wait about ten minutes before Ames' crew arrived.

And Ames arrived with a big crew. Jacobs secretly

hoped that Ames would come with just one or two men, even though he knew that was unlikely. Then Jacobs could spring out of the bushes and end this thing once and for all. But he knew it wouldn't be that easy. Ames must have expected some kind of trick, because it looked like he brought half of his gang with him.

Ten cars came through the gate. And all of them had at least four men inside. They parked in three rows. Ames' car was in the middle. Jacobs watched from the bushes as all the men piled out of their vehicles. He hoped he could get a clear shot at Ames, though the cars and men blocked his aim. He could see Ames walking to the car that the men were trapped inside the trunk of, but his sight line was off.

If this moment had been six months ago, he probably would have taken the shot and taken his chances afterward. But now Tiffany had entered his life, and if he had any hopes of ever having a normal life again, he needed her in it. And that meant not taking unnecessary or stupid chances. And this would probably qualify as both.

If there were only two or three men, his decision would be easy. He'd still take the shot. But with forty men in the vicinity, that would be suicide. It'd be unlikely he'd be able to get away. And with Tiffany now in his thoughts, he couldn't, and wouldn't, take that gamble.

Ames walked over to the car and stood just behind the trunk. "Open it up."

One of his men walked over to the driver's side to pop it open. Another of his men came over to Ames and stood in front of him.

"You should probably stand back, boss. Just in case."

Ames nodded and took a few steps back. Though if there were a bomb planted, it probably wouldn't have made much difference.

"Maybe you should go back in the car," the man said.

"Just open it," Ames said

The trunk popped open, and his guard went over to it and lifted it up fully. He looked inside and saw the two men lying in there. He looked back at Ames and waved at him to come look. Ames stepped forward and saw his men. He had a disgusted look on his face, but he wasn't really surprised by what he found. He expected something like that. Though he was a little surprised they were still alive.

"Get them out of there," Ames said.

As his team helped the men out of the trunk, Ames walked back over to his car. He leaned up against the front of his hood. He was now completely out of Jacobs' sight. The two men got out of the trunk and immediately went over to Ames' position.

"You two look like crap," Ames said.

Both men looked embarrassed. "Sorry, boss."

"What happened?"

"We went to the house like you told us. We looked around and didn't see anyone. So we went around the back. We were just about to get inside, then bam, out of nowhere, this guy shows up."

"Jacobs?"

"No, some other guy. Don't know who he was."

The look on Ames' face indicated he thought they were lying or crazy. "Some other guy? Franks?"

"No, somebody else. Never seen him before. He's not one of the people associated with Jacobs that you told us about."

"What'd he look like?"

"Big guy. Six-one, six-two, two hundred and something pounds, probably. Looked like a weightlifter or something. Or maybe a boxer or MMA fighter or something."

"And this guy, this one guy, took out the both of you?"

"We tried, boss, we really did. He was just... I mean, I dunno... he was just good."

Ames was getting angrier by the second. "So this one guy took out both of you? One guy?"

"Boss, we did our best. Really. He was just better."

Another of Ames' trusted men leaned over to him. "Who do you think this guy is, boss?"

"I don't know," Ames replied. "Maybe Jacobs sent out for some hired help."

"You want me to put the word out? See if we can find out who it is?"

"Yes. Do that."

"What else do we do about the Vogels?"

"Nothing for now. Not until we know who else we're dealing with. We'll come up with a new plan. One that Jacobs doesn't see coming."

9

Jacobs got home and was instantly greeted at the door by Tiffany and Gunner. Tiffany kissed him on the lips. Though he was pleased with the kiss, he thought he detected something troubling on her face.

"What is it? What's wrong?"

Tiffany smiled and waved her hand, trying to play it off. "Oh, it's... nothing."

"Don't do that. If we're gonna do this, let's not have any secrets, huh? Just say what's on your mind."

"OK." She took a deep breath, trying to figure out how she wanted to say what was thinking. "I'm... I don't want to be the anxious worrywart or anything, but I'm just glad you're here. Every time you walk out that door, I get a little scared that you're not coming back."

Jacobs took her in his arms and hugged her tight. "I'm not going anywhere."

They pulled away from each other, and Tiffany wiped a tear from her eye. "Like I said, I don't wanna be that nag or that person who's constantly... whatever... I'm just glad you're back."

"Hey. You don't have to worry. I can handle myself."

"I know you can."

"And now that I have you, I'm being extra careful. I won't get into anything unless I'm sure I'm walking out of it."

"You promise?"

"I promise. Besides, I couldn't leave you and Gunner dealing with Eddie all by yourselves. That's a punishment worse than death."

Tiffany laughed. "Hey, stop ragging on him all the time. He's..."

"Listen, he's a lot of things, and most of them he deserves to be ridiculed for, but I couldn't do this without him. He's always been there for me, and no matter what I say about him..." Jacobs looked away for a second, not wanting to say anymore.

"You care about him. Just say it."

"No."

"Just admit it."

"I... can't."

Tiffany kept laughing at his stubbornness to reveal his true feelings for his friend. "C'mon, just say it."

"Nope."

They both started laughing together, then went over to the couch when his phone rang. Jacobs looked at the number, and his mood instantly changed. The smile wiped off his face quickly as he prepared himself.

Right away, Tiffany recognized the problem. "What is it?"

Jacobs just shook his head, then answered the phone. "Yeah?"

Ames laughed. "It's so nice that we have this constant communication available to us now, isn't it?"

"What do you want?"

"I liked the little present you left for me. I'm a little surprised that they're still alive, but..."

"Is there a point you wanna make?"

"Not really. I just wanted to see if you were interested in meeting face-to-face."

"What for?"

"Maybe we can hash out our differences."

Jacobs laughed. "Yeah, right. You just wanna get me to a place where you can ambush me."

"I give you my word. No tricks."

"Well, we both know what your word is worth, don't we?"

"Now, now, there's no reason to resort to cheap shots, is there?"

"What do you really want?"

"I told you. I would just like a discussion with you."

"We're having it now."

"I like to look people in the eye."

"Oh yeah? Since when?"

"Do you want to keep going with the cheap shots, or do you want to possibly put our issues behind us?"

"I know you've got something up your sleeve."

"Brett, I'm simply asking you to meet so we can possibly put our differences aside. Wouldn't it be better to take that chance than have us killing each other? Or people we care about?"

"Depends."

"If you meet with me, we discuss things, maybe we can get on the same page. Then you can live in peace knowing that your girlfriend, her family, and you, are safe. And I can go on about my business without thinking that you're coming for me. Isn't that worth the risk for all of us?"

Jacobs still didn't trust the man. And he wasn't sure Ames deserved to have a truce. But for Tiffany and her family's sake, he thought he'd better listen. "Fine. I'll meet with you. But if you think I'm gonna walk into a meeting with you and have fifty of your cronies around, you've got another thing coming."

"Name the terms."

"I'll meet with you. One on one. Nobody else."

"I can agree to that. How about we make it a place that's on neutral turf? No, you know what? Just to show that I'm on the up-and-up, I'll even do it on your turn. How about we meet at the cemetery?"

"The cemetery? Why?"

"It's a place you know well, you're familiar with it..."

"And some of your boys tried to knock me off there the other day."

Ames laughed. "That was under our previous arrangement. If we come to an understanding here, there's no need to fear."

"Yeah, right. And we just happen to stand out there in the open, and you have a sniper nearby who gets to take a free shot at me? No thanks."

Ames laughed again. "So distrustful."

"You give me good reason to be."

"Perhaps. How about we do it like this? We'll meet at the cemetery right out in the open. I know you've got a friend out there who obviously has a set of skills himself, so bring him. Put him somewhere. Give him instructions that if you go down, so do I. That levels the playing field a little, doesn't it?"

"Maybe."

"If one of us gets hit, the other one's not getting away, which means we both have a reason for the other to literally walk away from this meeting."

"Possibly."

"So what do you say? Do we have a deal?"

"When did you wanna do this thing?"

"Since we're both obviously awake and in the moment, why not do it now?"

"Fine. I'll meet you there in thirty minutes."

"Sounds good. I hope we can come to some sort of arrangement."

Jacobs hung up and looked at Tiffany. She looked worried.

"What was that about?"

"Ames wants to meet."

Tiffany put a hand over her mouth, not liking the sound of that. "Oh no. You're not going to do it, are you?"

"Yeah."

"Brett, why? Why would you meet with him?"

"If there's a chance of us putting this behind us and getting you out of danger, I have to take that chance."

"Please, Brett, no. It's some sort of trick."

"It doesn't sound like a trick. He's willing to meet one on one, out in the open."

"He'll have someone there to shoot you."

"If I call Nathan and have him there to back me up, it'll be fine. Ames knows if someone shoots me, then someone's shooting him. He's not taking that kind of chance."

Tiffany had another horrifying thought. "What if it's just a ploy to get Nathan away from my parents? What if he's just doing this because he knows that will draw him away and give him a free shot to send someone else after them?"

Jacobs sighed. He hadn't thought of that, but he couldn't discount it either. It actually made perfect sense. He put his hand on his face and rubbed his cheeks as he thought about it. "No, you're right. We can't take that kind of chance. We'll have to leave Nathan where he is."

"So you're not going to go, right?"

"As stupid as it sounds, I have to."

"But why? You know he has no interest in actually letting us go."

"My inclination is that you're right. But maybe he says something I can use later on. Maybe I can get him to slip, say something I can use to my advantage."

"But if Nathan's not going, then you've got no backup."

"Sure I do."

"Who?"

"I'll call Eddie."

Tiffany pulled her head back, and her eyes widened. She loved Franks, but she also knew his limitations. "Brett, you know I love Eddie, but I also know he's not exactly..."

Jacobs grinned. "I know. But in this case, he'll do. I don't actually expect him to need to do anything, anyway. Besides, I'll have my vest on just in case. Everything will be fine."

"Take Gunner with you."

Jacobs shook his head. "No. I want him here with

you, just in case. If you were here alone, I'd worry. But if he's here, I know you're protected."

Tiffany took a deep breath. She didn't like anything that she was hearing. But she also knew that Jacobs wasn't changing his mind. And he did know more about this type of stuff than she did. She just had to trust that he knew what he was doing. And that he'd come back to her.

10
___

Jacobs pulled into a parking spot at the cemetery. He already had his gun out in case it was a trap. Before getting out of the car, he looked around for signs of trouble, though he didn't see any. It was dark, so it'd be tough to see even if there was something there. Jacobs put his ear comm in and tested it.

"You hear me, Eddie?"

"Loud and clear, man."

"I'm gonna get out now. You see Ames yet?"

"Well, I see someone standing out there. Wait, let me look through this scope." Franks looked through the scope on his rifle and got a clear view of Ames' face. "Yeah, that's him, man. I gotta say I'm surprised. I didn't think he'd actually show."

"Maybe he's on the level after all."

"Fat chance, man. If he's on the level, then I'm getting ready to step on the moon."

"You need bigger boots."

"You know what I'm saying. Hey, before you move in, you sure you wanna do this?"

"Pretty sure it's too late now," Jacobs said.

"It's never too late. It's only too late when you're dead. Then it's way too late. But now? Not even close."

"Well, I'm going anyway."

"What if Tiff was right? What if this was just a way to lure you and Nathan out, then have them swing down on her parents again?"

"Well then, I guess they're gonna have a nasty surprise waiting for them."

Franks laughed. "Yeah, I guess they will. Sure would be nice to see that."

"I'm going in."

"Wait, before you do that."

"How many times are you gonna hold me up?"

"Just one more time."

"What now?"

"You do realize I'm not the greatest of shots, right?"

"I'm fully aware."

"So if something goes down, I may or may not hit what I'm aiming for."

"Just do the best you can."

"OK. Just wanted to make sure we're clear on that."

"I'm well aware of your limitations, believe me. And I don't think it matters what kind of shot you are. It just matters that Ames believes there's someone out there who's capable of hitting him."

"OK, because I have improved and all somewhat, but—"

"Eddie?"

"Yeah?"

"Can I go now?"

"Oh, yeah, sorry. Go ahead."

"Remember, just keep that gun pointed right at Ames. Nothing else. I'll take care of anything else. Don't get distracted. You've got one target. Keep it on him."

"Will do, man, will do."

Jacobs walked through the parking lot, and onto the grass that led to the graves. He saw the outline of a man standing in front of the graves of his family. He kept his head spinning all around, just in case there was someone lying in the weeds, hoping to sneak up on him. He reached Ames without incident. Ames turned around to face him as he heard Jacobs coming.

"Glad you were able to make it."

"Start talking," Jacobs said. He wasn't in the mood for small talk.

Ames had his own agenda, though. He looked back at the graves. "Sad, isn't it? The loss of innocent lives. Tragic."

"Yeah."

"It's amazing when you think about it, isn't it? How one life is affected by so many others. We tend to think of ourselves as individuals, but that's not really true. We're all affected by so many others."

Ames had another of his men waiting in another car in the parking lot. He'd gotten down low in the back seat, making sure he kept out of sight. As Ames and Jacobs were talking, the man snuck out of the car, keeping low to the ground, and went over to Jacobs' car. He put a tracking device under the back bumper, then slithered away to his own vehicle again.

Ames' only true motive was to keep Jacobs there long enough for his man to achieve his goal. "So, I assume we both have guns pointed at each other, correct?"

"I'd say that's likely."

Ames nodded. "Then I guess we should make this short and sweet then."

"That's how I prefer it."

"As I mentioned, I would like to call a truce between us."

"Why?"

"Because it's a war I'm not sure either of us can win. Besides, there are bigger things about to come into play."

"Such as?"

"Well, I still have Butch to contend with. And he's being a pain in my side as well. Then there's the matter of Mallette."

Jacobs tilted his head and made a face upon hearing that name. "What?"

"Haven't you heard?"

"Heard what?"

"He's got a new lawyer."

"So? He's had them before."

"Yes, but I hear this one might actually have something."

"Like what?"

"I'm not sure. But I'm hearing rumblings that the guy might actually be able to get Mallette out early."

Jacobs wasn't sure how he felt about that. Sad that Mallette wouldn't be serving all the time he deserved, or happy that he might finally get a crack at him.

Ames continued. "In any case, if there's a chance he might get out early, then that means one more person I'll have to deal with. So you see, I simply want you out of the way as quickly as possible."

"Why the sudden change? I'm sure you didn't just find out all this information in the last two hours."

"Maybe seeing my two men in the trunk of a car made me realize that I was fighting a losing battle. You obviously have more help than I realized. Maybe I was too hasty in trying to eliminate you."

Ames seemed genuine, but Jacobs still wasn't sure he was buying it yet. Words didn't mean a whole lot to him these days. Actions meant more. What he needed to do was see if he could pull any nuggets of information out of him that Jacobs might be able to use later if he wasn't as genuine as he seemed.

"If you wanna take on Mallette if he ever gets out, and Butch at the same time, you might wanna add some troops to your arsenal. Because I gotta tell you, the people you've hired so far don't exactly seem like the cream of the crop."

"I've got fifty or sixty men. I think I'll be fine."

Jacobs shook his head. "If you wanna take on Mallette, take it from experience, you're gonna need more. Because I guarantee you that while he's been in prison, he's already been putting his team together. And he's gonna hit the street running."

Ames grinned. "Thanks for the concern. But I think we'll be OK."

"Suit yourself. But I know the man. And right now, when he gets out, his number one target isn't gonna be me. It's gonna be you."

"And why is that?"

"Because he views himself as the man in charge of this city. And when he gets out and sees that you're sitting in his chair, you're gonna be the first on his hit list. So you better be ready."

Ames continued his grin. "Well, thank you for the concern. I'll be sure to keep my guard up."

"Hope wherever you've got yourself bunkered in at... hope you're adequately protected."

"I'm not particularly worried about it. But again, thank you for your concern," Ames said.

"If you want to give me the addresses of some of your places, I could check them out for you, make sure they're not easily penetrable for Mallette if he ever tries to make a move on them."

Ames knew exactly what Jacobs was doing. It was

the same thing he would be doing in reverse. Hell, it was the same thing he was doing now by putting a tracking device under Jacobs' car. But he was taking the bait.

"I've got my own security team for that."

"Suit yourself."

"So, do we have an agreement?" Ames asked, sticking his hand out to shake.

Jacobs looked down at Ames' hand. He had no intention of ever shaking hands with him. Not if they were friends. Not if they were enemies. Jacobs then raised his eyes level and looked at Ames in the eyes. "For now."

"For now?" Ames lowered his hand. "Is there something else I have to do?"

"Yeah. You have to earn my trust. And you haven't yet."

"What do I have to do to earn that?"

"You'll know it when you do."

Ames nodded. "So, I guess we have a temporary truce then? Until it becomes a permanent one?"

"We'll see how it goes."

Jacobs had nothing else to say and didn't think Ames was going to stumble and spill anything worth hanging around for, so he turned and started leaving.

"Look forward to eventually standing side by side," Ames said.

Jacobs heard him, but didn't want to give a reply, and kept on walking. Within a few minutes, he was back in his car. Before turning the car on, he contacted Franks.

"How are you doing up there?"

"Hey, man, ain't gotta ask me. Question is, how you doing?"

"Fine. Did you hear all that nonsense?"

"Oh yeah."

"What'd you think?"

"I think that's a man that's got something up his sleeve, that's what I think."

"Did you hear that part about Mallette?"

"Yeah, I heard it. Don't know if it's true, though. I haven't heard anything about it," Franks said.

"Just the same, might be something worth looking into."

"Yeah, I'll do some digging on it tomorrow. See what I can turn up."

"OK. You didn't notice anything funny while I was out there, did you?"

"Like what?"

"I don't know. Like anything."

"Well, you told me to keep my eyes on Ames, so that's what I did. I wasn't looking around for anything else."

"Fair enough. I'm gonna call Nathan and make sure he doesn't have company."

"Sounds good. I take it I'm able to leave here now?"

"Yeah, go ahead."

"All right. I'll talk to you tomorrow."

Jacobs then took out his phone and dialed Thrower, making sure that this wasn't some type of diversion in order to get an easier path at Tiffany's parents. Thrower picked up right away.

"Nate, how you looking there? All good?"

"Everything's safe and sound that I can see," Thrower replied.

"Good. Glad to see that my fears about this meeting weren't warranted. Guess he wasn't trying to pull you away."

"Well, there's still time if he thinks I'm still with you."

"Yeah, you're right about that. Just keep your eyes open, huh?"

"Always do."

Jacobs started his car and drove away. As he drove off, Ames reached his vehicle. The driver opened the back door for him. Once he was inside, the man got behind the wheel.

"Did you get it done?" Ames asked.

"All done, sir. It's on the vehicle."

"Excellent. Now, we'll finally be able to do what we've failed at so far."

"With respect, sir, why not just put a bomb on the car and take out Jacobs while we're able?"

"A few days ago and that would have been the smart play. But now, with this new guy he's got working with him, he's obviously enlarging his team. There's more at play here than just Jacobs. There's his girlfriend, Franks, this new guy; I want to be able to take them all out. If we just take out Jacobs now, there are still the others."

"Understood."

"Don't worry. Jacobs' turn will come soon enough."

11

Jacobs had just returned to his house, surprised to see Franks greeting him by the door.

"What are you doing here?" Jacobs asked.

Tiffany jumped up from the couch and answered for him. "I asked him to come. I was a little nervous waiting here by myself. I mean, I know Gunner was here, but still."

Jacobs smiled at her. "It's fine."

"Question is, why am I here before you?" Franks asked. "We both left at around the same time."

"I drove over and met with Nate. He said everything was fine when I called him, but I guess I just wanted to see for myself. Make sure Tiff's parents were OK."

Tiffany smiled at him. "Thank you for that. Everything's OK?"

"Yeah, everything's fine."

"I'm so glad."

"Nothing to worry about tonight."

"Eddie told me about the meeting. Seems kind of strange, don't you think?"

Franks agreed. "Yeah, the more I've been thinking about it, the more I'm inclined to think something's up."

"Such as?" Jacobs asked.

"I dunno, man. Just seems off."

"Could be. But without having specifics, I'm not gonna worry about it tonight. Besides, you got some homework to do in the morning."

"I do?"

"Yeah. About a certain someone."

"Mallette?" Tiffany asked.

Jacobs looked at her, not wanting to confirm it, but not willing to lie about it either. "Yeah."

"Is it ever going to end for you?"

"It will. I just need to sort things out first."

"OK. Well, since you're back, I'm gonna go to bed now." Tiffany leaned over and kissed him. "Goodnight." She then retreated to her bedroom.

Franks pointed to the hallway she just disappeared from. "Hey, are you two gonna…"

"Would you stop?" Jacobs replied.

"What? It's a legitimate question."

"We got more important things to think about."

"Oh, you mean like what Ames' real goal was about meeting tonight?"

"Yeah. Like that."

They threw around some ideas, though they couldn't come up with anything concrete. At this point, Ames could have been up to just about anything. But after thirty minutes of discussing it, Jacobs was about done for the night.

"Let's kick it around more tomorrow. I'm tired."

"What do you want me to do about the Mallette thing?" Franks asked.

"Find out if there's even a one percent chance that maniac might get out early."

Franks nodded. "All right, will do. Are you actually gonna get some rest tonight or are you gonna curl up with..."

"Would you just get out of here?"

The following morning, Jacobs and Tiffany had just eaten their breakfast when his phone rang. He answered it after seeing it was Franks, assuming he had some news for him, possibly involving Mallette.

"Hey, you got anything?"

"Oh, I got something, man," Franks replied.

"What?"

"Word has it that Ames has a meeting going down in like two hours."

"Where?"

"One of his usual hangouts."

"Who's he meeting with?"

"Word I got is he's got a big drug shipment that he's picking up. Could be worth millions."

"Millions, huh?" Jacobs thought about it for a second. "Sounds like something that could really hurt him if something happened to that shipment."

"Could be. And the rumor is that he's gonna be at this meeting personally to make sure everything goes according to plan."

"How reliable is this information?"

"I mean, comes from the usual sources, man. I got no reason to doubt it. But just like always, can't ever guarantee anything. My source is right more times than not, but..."

"Yeah, yeah, I know. Can you double check everything, contact a few other sources to see if they've heard anything?"

"Man, who you think you're talking to? I already done all that."

"And?"

"I don't have any other confirmation besides the one source. But you know how it goes. That ain't unusual when you're talking about the kinds of people we're dealing with. They don't exactly go around advertising it to every chump that walks the street, you know?"

"Yeah."

"I mean, if you think it's no good, that's cool. I just wanted to let you know it's out there."

"No, it is what it is."

"The source I got it from is good. Now, whether he got it from a reputable source too, I can't say."

"Regardless, it's something we gotta check out."

"That's why I'm bringing it to you."

"All right, thanks. Text me the address to that place so I can check it out."

"You got it."

Jacobs hung up the phone and immediately felt Tiffany's stare. He looked over at her.

"I'm assuming you're leaving soon?"

Jacobs nodded. "Could be something... could be something that brings Ames to his knees."

Tiffany plastered on a smile, though she was more sad than anything. "I understand."

"I'm sorry, it's just..."

"You don't have to apologize for anything. I understand. You've done everything you can to keep me safe. I get it."

Jacobs opened his mouth to say something, then closed it before any words came out. "If there's even the slightest chance that this could be something that frees the both of us, I gotta look into it."

"I know. I told you... I get it. And I do. I really do. Just... whenever you get there. Be safe."

"I will. I'll leave Gunner here like usual, and..."

"No." Tiffany shook her head. "If this is really something that could finally finish this, then I want you to take him with you. You'll need him more than I do. And he'd help you accomplish that."

"But I also want you to be safe."

"Brett, I'm fine. Nobody knows we're here. If you're gone for a few hours, I'll be fine. Besides, if Ames and his men are elsewhere, then there's nothing to worry about here."

Jacobs still wasn't sure it was the best idea. It was written all over his face that he was hesitant about leaving her alone.

"I don't know. I still..."

"Brett." Tiffany put her hand on his. "If this could really end it, you could probably use his help. I'll be fine. Really. I want you to take him. He'll help keep you safe, and I'll worry less about you if he's with you. Take him. Please."

It was still against his better judgment, but he really couldn't argue against her logic. Things certainly would be easier and better for him if Gunner was at his side. But he still didn't like the idea of leaving Tiffany alone.

"I could always have Nate swing by to make sure you're OK."

Tiffany shook her head. "No. Keep him at my parents. They need his protection more than I do." She then flashed him a more natural smile. "I'll be fine. OK?"

Jacobs finally agreed with her position. He looked

over at Gunner. "You ready to get back in the swing of things?"

Gunner barked. He was more than ready. Jacobs took a few more minutes to get ready, then looked at his phone and saw that Franks had texted him the address. Jacobs looked the address up, seeing that it would take him about thirty or forty minutes to get there.

"I gotta leave soon," Jacobs said. "I'll get there about an hour before them, then I can survey everything and pick my spot."

Tiffany leaned over and gave him a kiss. "Just make sure it's a good one."

Jacobs and Gunner had been waiting at the meeting spot for the past hour. Jacobs walked around for a bit first to pick out the spot he liked best. And he thought he had a good one. He was on the first floor of a nearby vacant building. Once Ames arrived, he should have had a pretty good shot at him. And if things got too heavy after that, he had an escape path lined up already.

Everything looked like it would go his way, assuming that Ames was actually there. That turned out to be a big if. The meeting time came and went, with no sign of anyone. Jacobs looked at his watch. It was now twenty minutes past. Gunner let out a bark.

"Yeah, I know, buddy. I'm beginning to think this was some bad info too."

Gunner growled.

"We'll give it a little more time."

Gunner let out a deeper sounding growl and lay down.

"I don't know. Another half hour, maybe."

Gunner kept making sounds, indicating his displeasure with the wait. After another thirty minutes, Jacobs knew nobody was coming.

"Looks like we've been had on this one."

Gunner finally perked up and sat again.

"I think it's time to leave, buddy."

Gunner barked a couple times.

"I don't know if it was done intentionally. But it sure makes you wonder, doesn't it?"

12

Tiffany looked out the window. It'd been half an hour since Jacobs and Gunner left. She didn't know why, but she was feeling uneasy. It was the first time in the last couple months that she'd been by herself. At least at the house. Every other time Jacobs left, he kept Gunner behind. She wasn't sure why she was so nervous. In her mind, there was no reason to be. But there she was, staring out the window, looking for something that didn't seem right.

Since everything seemed fine, Tiffany went over to the table and picked her book up, then went over to the couch and sat down to start reading. She read a couple of pages, then picked her head up and looked at the door. She looked at the window, then turned her head to look at the hallway and the kitchen. She shook her head to get the scary thoughts out of her head and went back to reading.

Outside were two separate cars, both having two men inside. They were all employed by Ames. They were at separate ends of the parking lot, but they each had a view of the front door of Jacobs' place. The leader of the four was a man nicknamed Sludge. He called Ames to get further instructions.

"Boss, Jacobs and his dog left about thirty minutes ago. What do you want us to do?"

"Who's still there?" Ames asked.

"Just the girl."

"You're sure she's there?"

"Positive. We saw her at the door and close it as Jacobs left. She's there. No doubt about it."

"And she's alone?"

"We've been watching since last night. Nobody else has gone in. And only Jacobs and the dog have come out."

"OK. I want you to go in."

"Should we wait for Jacobs to come back first?"

"No. That might be a little more complicated. If you wait for him, you'll have him, the dog, and the girl to contend with. Plus, if you break in, there's no telling if Jacobs will shoot the lot of you as you get in. You might not ever even get to him. Get in there now. Take care of the girl. Then you'll sit there and wait for Jacobs to get home. You can surprise him as he walks through the door. Then you can take out him and the dog before they know what hit them."

"What do you want us to do with the girl?"

Ames didn't hesitate. "Kill her."

"You don't want us to bring her somewhere?"

"No. I want her dead. Do you have a problem doing it?"

"No, boss. Just wanted to make sure."

"In the event that Jacobs somehow manages to elude us again, losing another person that's significant to him might just bring him to his knees. We might not ever have to deal with him again. The toll of another woman getting killed because of him might just shove him over the edge. He'll end up in a straitjacket. Kill her. As violently as possible."

Sludge looked at his partner briefly. "You got it, boss."

"Let me know when it's done."

Sludge put the phone down and looked at his partner again. "Looks like it's go time."

The two men got out of the car and started walking towards Jacobs' place. Sludge motioned to the men in the other car to start moving in. They'd go in through the back. Tiffany was still on the couch, reading her book. She was just starting to calm her nerves and put her mind at ease as she got more into the book. Then there was a knock on the door.

Tiffany jumped out of her seat, the book shuffling off her lap and onto the couch. She let out a slight noise but quickly put her hand over her mouth in hopes of muffling any sound she might not realize she was making. She sat there, frozen, not moving a muscle. She stared at the door. She could only hope it was some salesperson going door-to-door, and they'd move on after a few seconds. Her heart was beating fast. It felt like it skipped a few beats. She started breathing heavier.

Then there were a few more knocks. A lump went down Tiffany's throat as she figured out what to do. There were a couple more knocks. They were getting louder. So were the beats in her chest. She started biting her lip.

If there was one thing that Jacobs tried to beat into her head over the past couple months was that if he wasn't there, she wasn't to open the door for anyone. Not even Franks. And nobody else knew she was there.

"Tiffany!" Sludge shouted through the door. "Tiffany! Open up!"

Tiffany put both hands over her mouth, alarmed to hear her name called. How did they know her name? Jacobs told her he would never send anyone there for her. He didn't trust anyone enough to do that, other than Franks. And that was not Franks' voice.

"Tiffany! Brett sent us over to get you. Please open up."

She started looking around, wondering where she should go. She had to get away. She had to hide. She jumped off the couch and ran to the back of the house and peeked out the corner of the window. She was horrified to see two men standing near the back door.

"Oh my god, oh my god," she whispered. "What am I gonna do?"

She hurried back through the house, when she suddenly heard thumping on the door. It sounded like they were trying to break it down.

"Tiffany, we know you're in there!"

She put her hands on her head and frantically looked around, not sure where she should go. She ran into the hallway. She still wasn't sure where she was going. She then found herself in the bathroom. She locked the door. She quickly looked around, hoping she could put something in front of the door to prevent them from breaking through it. There was nothing, though.

Tiffany jumped when she heard a loud bang. It was the sound of the men breaking through the front door. She started looking through the medicine cabinet, hoping she could find something she might be able to use to protect herself. She couldn't find anything.

Not knowing what else to do, she looked at the bathtub and jumped in it. There was a window just above it. The only chance she had now was to climb through it. As she fiddled with the window, she was startled when she heard the knob of the door jiggle. She turned back around, horrified to see that the door started moving. They were trying to break it down. She quickly went back to the window.

Just as Tiffany got it opened, the door broke open, with two men rushing in. She looked back and let out a scream, desperately trying to jump up and climb through the window. The two men hurried over to her and grabbed hold of her, dragging her out of the bathtub. Tiffany let out a few screams and tried breaking free from the grasp of the two men, but it was to no avail. She even tried kicking her way out, but she just couldn't get loose. The two men dragged her into the living room.

"What now?" one of the men asked.

Sludge responded. "Boss said he wanted it done as violently as possible."

"Rape her first?"

Sludge shrugged. "Do what you want. Just make it fast. I don't wanna be caught with our pants down if Jacobs suddenly shows up. Just hurry it up. Then we'll slap her around a bit, maybe carve her up a bit, then we'll put a bullet in her head."

Tiffany continued screaming, hoping someone would hear her and come to her rescue. Hearing what they had planned for her, she wasn't going to go down without a fight. As two of the men held her arms out, one of the men got on top of her.

"Please!" Tiffany yelled.

Suddenly, the front door swung open. Thrower ran into the room at full speed, launching his body at Sludge who was the only one standing. Thrower quickly got up, threw a punch at Sludge's face, then turned around to face the rest of the men, who had now let go of Tiffany.

Thrower didn't wait for the other men to make the first move. Outnumbered as he was, he was going on the offensive. That was always his strategy when the odds weren't in his favor. If he waited, that gave his opponents the upper hand. He had to put them on the defensive and give himself the advantage.

Thrower charged at the man on his right, spearing him in the gut and taking him down. As they wrestled on the ground, the other men came over. That gave Tiffany time to crawl away. She leaned up against the far wall and watched for a second.

The other two men picked Thrower up, grabbing each of his arms, holding him at bay for the third man to work him over. As the man got back to his feet and walked over to him, Thrower gave him a thrust kick between his legs. As the man hunched over, Thrower was able to wiggle his wrist free from the one man on his left. He then gave him a quick left hook, spun down on the ground and kicked out the legs of the remaining man, sending him down to the ground as well.

Thrower quickly looked back at Tiffany. "Get out of here."

"What about you?"

"Don't worry about me. Get out."

Tiffany got up and ran out the door. Thrower turned his attention back to the men, just in time to receive a punch to the side of his face, sending him stumbling backwards. Thrower steadied himself, then the two men started trading punches. Within a few seconds, Thrower started to get the upper hand. Out of the corner of his eye, though, he saw Sludge standing in the corner of the room, pointing a gun at him.

Reacting quickly, and on instinct, Thrower grabbed the man he was fighting, and put his arm around his throat, then used his positioning to slide around to the man's back. Just as Sludge opened fire, Thrower yanked the other man in front of him, using him as a shield. Sludge emptied his gun into the man's chest. Thrower kept the man in front of him for a second, then let the body fall to the floor.

Thrower ran towards Sludge and launched himself at him again. He threw a punch that landed on Sludge's head at the same time as he reached him. Sludge's back and head slammed into the wall. He was a little shaky as Thrower began his assault.

The man who got kicked in the groin finally made it back to his feet. He took out a knife and threw it at Thrower. Thrower yelled in agony as he felt the sharp steel blade lodge into his left leg. He looked down at it, and without thinking, yanked it out of his leg. Swapping it into his right hand, he then reached back, and threw it back at the man who it belonged to.

The man screamed in pain as the blade went into the middle of his chest. He stood there for a second, in shock that it happened, then dropped to his knees. He fell over onto his side. With Thrower distracted, Sludge belted him on the back of the head, sending Thrower to his hands and knees on the ground.

"Who are you?!" Sludge asked, putting his hands on Thrower's head to pick him back up.

"Your nightmare," Thrower replied. He instantly started nailing Sludge with punches to his midsection, alternating between his left and right hands. He was going so fast it looked like Thrower was using the man as a speed bag.

The other man who remained, besides Sludge, came along and put all his weight into slugging Thrower in the back. Thrower lost his balance and was forced into Sludge, both of them going down to the ground. As he rested on top of Sludge, Thrower put his hand on the left side of the man's waist, feeling the handle of a knife. In one swift motion, Thrower removed the knife, rolled over, and shoved the blade into the man's midsection.

The man stood there for a moment, stunned at what just happened. As blood started pouring out of his stomach and onto the floor, he dropped to his knees. Thrower got to his feet, then watched as the man fell over onto his side. Sludge also got to his feet. The two remaining men just stood there, several feet apart, each of them looking at the other.

"Looks like it's just us now," Sludge said.

"Seems so."

With his weapons now gone, there was only one thing Sludge could do. He put his hands up, ready for a fight. Thrower tried to ignore the pain in his leg the best he could, and put his hands up as well. Sludge took a few steps in his opponent's direction.

"Who the hell are you, anyway?"

"Just call me The Bodyguard."

"That's gonna look a little funny on your tombstone." Sludge threw a left jab that missed.

Thrower responded with a kick from his good leg, though he winced a little, feeling the pain from standing on the bad one. Sludge mostly blocked it with his arm, anyway. Judging by the force he used with it, Thrower determined that if he was going to win this fight, he'd have to do it with his hands.

"You know what's gonna look funny on yours?" Thrower asked.

"What's that?"

"They're gonna write down that you died like a bitch."

Sludge immediately replied with a right hand that connected across the side of Thrower's face. Wanting to seize on the opportunity, Sludge lunged forward and got in close, grabbing Thrower around his neck. The two men wrestled for a few seconds before they both finally went down to the ground.

They continued wrestling, both of them getting in a few shots on the other. They tried punches, knees, elbows, anything they could to get a leg up on the other one. After a few minutes, though, Thrower used his superior combat skills to eventually slide around to Sludge's back.

Thrower put his arm around Sludge's neck, choking the life out of him. And he wasn't letting go until he felt the life drain out of Sludge's body. Sludge tried fighting it. He slapped and punched at Thrower's arm, kicked at him, scratched, everything he could think of to wiggle free. But he just couldn't do it. Thrower's grip was locked in tight.

Slowly, Sludge's movements indicated that he was losing the battle. His punches and kicks were becoming weaker with every second. After what seemed like an eternity, Sludge's body finally went limp. There was no more fight within him. Thrower kept his grip locked on for a few extra seconds, just to make sure that the man was really dead. Once Thrower was sure Sludge's time had expired, he let Sludge loose. He immediately fell to his side. Thrower felt the man's neck. He was dead.

Thrower slid back away from the dead body, giving himself a little room as he took some deep breaths. He looked around at what was left of the carnage. Four dead bodies. As the adrenaline started to die down, he put his hand on his leg, the pain becoming more intense.

Thrower then grabbed Sludge's arm and tore the sleeve right off of his shirt. He then wrapped it around his leg to stop the bleeding. Knowing he had to start moving, Thrower stood up and started walking for the door. As he reached it, he looked back at his victims.

Considering what they were planning on doing, he had no sympathy for them.

Thrower walked out of the house, limping. As he walked down the steps, Tiffany ran over to him. Seeing that he was hurt, she put his arm around her so she could help him walk.

"I thought I told you to get out?"

"I did," Tiffany replied. "I was waiting over there by the cars. I couldn't just leave without knowing what happened to you."

"Oh."

Tiffany looked back at the house. "What happened to them?"

"You won't have to worry about them anymore."

"I'm so sorry this happened to you."

Thrower seemed unaffected by his injury, though he was touched by her concern. "All part of the job. Let's get to my car over there."

"Thank you so much for helping me."

"You're welcome."

"If it wasn't for you…"

"Don't even finish the sentence. Don't think or worry about what might have happened. All that matters is what did. And now you're safe."

"I'll never be able to repay you."

"You don't have to."

Once they finally reached the car, Tiffany helped Thrower get in the back seat so he could stretch his leg out, while she got behind the wheel. She peeled out of the parking lot, though she wasn't sure where she was going. She reached for her phone, then realized she didn't have it.

"Oh, no, I don't have my phone."

"Use mine," Thrower said. "It's there on the passenger seat."

Tiffany reached over and grabbed it, then scrolled to Franks' number. She didn't want to call Jacobs in case he was busy with something, and she didn't want to distract him if he was. Franks was the next best bet. He immediately picked up.

"Eddie, we're in trouble."

"Slow down, slow down, what's wrong?" Franks asked.

Tiffany then told him everything that had happened. "What am I supposed to do?"

"Just relax. Relax. I'll send someone over there right now to clean up the scene."

"How are you gonna clean that up?"

"Well, clean it up as in getting everything out of there that might identify you. The bodies are staying. It's probably too late to get them out without being noticed. But I can have someone there in five minutes to do the rest."

"What about Nathan? Should I take him to the hospital?"

"No. Don't worry. I got a guy."

13

Jacobs barged through the front door, surprised that it wasn't locked. Gunner ran in front of him, going into the living room. When Jacobs got there, Tiffany ran over to him, giving him the biggest hug she could muster. Jacobs put his arms around her and held her tight. He put his face into her hair, getting as close to her as possible. He'd almost lost her. He knew it. It had almost happened again. And if it wasn't for Thrower, it'd be a dramatically different scene right now. They pulled away from each other, looking into each other's eyes.

"I'm sorry."

Tiffany put her index finger in the air. "Don't you do that. Don't you even think about it."

"It's my fault."

"Brett, I don't want to hear that again. Stop. It was not your fault."

"She's right, man, stop doing that to yourself," Franks said. "All's well that ends well." Franks looked down at Thrower, who was sitting on the couch with his leg up. "Well, sort of speaking, if you know what I mean. I mean, not in your case."

Thrower looked up at him and smiled. "It's all good."

Jacobs looked at him, then walked over to him and shook hands. "Thank you so much. I owe you."

Thrower shook his head. "All part of the job. I'm just glad I was able to get there in time."

"So am I."

"That was a good call you had, having me roll over there just to make sure everything was good."

"I'm glad I did. I don't know what I would have done if..." Jacobs ran his hand over the back of his head. He didn't want to even finish the thought. "So what happened exactly?"

Thrower looked over at Tiffany and raised his arm slightly, having her start it since he wasn't there for the beginning. Tiffany then told him everything, exactly as it happened. Once she was done, Thrower chimed in with his version after he arrived.

"Bodies are still there?" Jacobs asked.

"Yeah, but don't worry, man," Franks replied. "I got someone in there already. They cleaned the place out, wiped it down, grabbed valuables and belongings and all that. So there's nothing there to identify either of you, but you'll have to get a new place."

"Wonderful."

"It's a good thing my guys got there when they did, too. Police showed up about half an hour after they left."

Jacobs shook his head. "How'd they know? How'd they know we were there?"

"Maybe you got followed?" Franks asked.

"No. I'm very careful, you know that. If I even think there's a five percent chance I'm being tailed, I'll go in another direction until I'm sure."

"They didn't just pick the house out of the blue," Thrower said. "They got tipped off somehow."

"Yeah, but how?" Jacobs looked at Tiffany. "Did you go anywhere? Text anyone where you were? Post a picture on social media? Tell your parents? Anything?"

Tiffany shook her head. "No. I swear. I haven't done anything. You can check my phone."

Jacobs gave her a smile and put his hand on her arm. "I believe you. I just don't know how they could've found us."

"Funny how they did it when you weren't there," Thrower said. "Almost like they knew you weren't."

Jacobs looked at him and kept nodding as he thought about it. "Yeah. Almost like they knew."

"What about my parents?" Tiffany asked, fearing for their safety, believing they were now unprotected with Thrower being there with them.

"It's all good, Tiff," Franks said. "I got someone else keeping an eye on them until he heals up again."

"I'm good now," Thrower said, standing up.

"You're not good," Tiffany said. "Sit down and relax. You've earned the time."

"There's people out there to protect. I can relax sitting in a car."

Tiffany wasn't going to give in. "You'll also not be moving too well."

"I'm fine."

"She's right there, Throw-bomb." Franks then began laughing hysterically. "Throw-bomb! You like it?" He started slapping his knee. "I just thought of that one right now. Throw-bomb. Ha! What do you think?"

Thrower stood there looking at him with a stoic face. He simply shook his head. "I don't think so."

"No, huh?"

Thrower grinned. "No."

"Oh. Well, uh, I'll keep working on that for you."

"My parents?" Tiffany asked.

"Oh, yeah, right. Almost forgot. Not to worry. Anyway, I got someone else watching them right now."

"You said that already," Jacobs said.

"I did?"

"Yes."

"Oh. Well, I got someone there."

Jacobs rolled his eyes. "We know!"

"Oh. Well then, what are you asking for?"

"Who is it?"

"Oh. You wanna know who it is?"

"Yes!"

"Oh. Well, why didn't you just say so instead of beating around the bush?" Jacobs put his hand on his forehead. He had nothing else to say. "Well, anyways, I actually put two guys there. Not as good as Nate here, but I think they'll be OK."

"What makes you think that?"

"They both did some amateur wrestling and boxing and stuff. They know how to handle themselves."

"But do they know how to handle themselves if someone's shooting at them?"

"They'll be fine, man, believe me. This ain't their first rodeo."

Jacobs sighed, but put his trust in Franks. "OK."

"So what do we do now?" Tiffany asked.

"Well, I guess we gotta work on finding us a new place first."

"I'm already working on that," Franks said. "Hopefully hear something before the day's over."

Tiffany went over to Jacobs and put her head into his chest. "Brett, when is this gonna end?"

He put his arms around her and his hand on the back of her head. "Soon. I promise. It'll end soon."

"Well, it might end sooner if we can figure out how they found you," Franks said.

Jacobs took his arms off of Tiffany. "Well, if she hasn't been out of the house other than with me, that leaves two options."

Franks looked down at Gunner. "Him?"

Gunner immediately barked at him.

"OK, OK. I don't think it's him either. You happy?"

Gunner barked again.

"No. It's either you or me," Jacobs said to Franks.

"Me? What makes you think it's me?"

"Tiffany hasn't been out unless I'm with her. Nathan was never at the house before, so the only way they could've done it is if they followed you or me."

"Oh. I get it. You're saying it was me, aren't you?"

Jacobs shrugged. "I'm careful."

"And I'm not?"

"You have been known to slip up from time to time."

"That don't mean it was me this time. Where's your proof?"

"It's not a court of law here."

"No, it's the Court of Eddie. And my ruling is that it wasn't me."

"Is that your final verdict?"

"Yes!"

"I dunno. Maybe it was me. Maybe I got sloppy. Wasn't paying attention one time," Jacobs said.

"It's gonna be hard to figure it out at this point," Thrower said. "Best thing to do now is just move on and keep plugging away."

"Yeah."

Gunner let out a slight growl, then ran into another room. Jacobs looked concerned. That was usually a clue that Gunner was onto something. They then heard an even louder growl. Jacobs knew what that meant. Someone was there.

"Why's he acting like that?" Tiffany asked.

"There's something wrong," Jacobs replied.

"What is it?"

"I don't know." He looked over Franks and gave Tiffany a slight nudge to walk in his direction. "Eddie."

Franks nodded, putting his arms out and waving at Tiffany to get behind him. Jacobs then looked at Thrower, who was already putting a magazine into his pistol. Jacobs looked back at Tiffany again.

"Is there someplace you can take her?"

"Basement?" Franks said.

Jacobs nodded. "Do it."

"Come on." Franks took Tiffany by the hand and hurried into the hallway, opening the door that led to the basement.

Jacobs and Thrower stood perfectly still, trying to hear any little sounds of movement. They also let their eyes roam between the windows and the door to see if they could make out shadows or a person's outline. Gunner came back into the room, still growling, though he was looking all around.

"How sure are we something's there?" Thrower asked.

"Hundred percent. He doesn't growl like that for no reason."

"Could it be someone just walking past?"

"No. He senses something," Jacobs said. "Trust me. Something's out there."

"What are they waiting for?"

"Probably us to stick our head out a window or something."

"Ames' men."

"Gotta be."

"How'd they find us here?"

"Another unanswered question right now," Jacobs replied.

They waited another minute, still not hearing anything. It was deathly quiet, outside of Gunner's growling. He kept going from room to room.

"Why does he keep moving?" Thrower asked.

"He's not sure where the danger is. Could mean that whoever's out there is moving."

"Or that there's more than one."

"Possible."

"Maybe you go out the front, and I'll go out the back. See if we can squeeze them off?"

"I don't know."

Jacobs wasn't fond of giving them a target, especially without knowing exactly where they were. But he also knew that they couldn't stay there indefinitely. If someone was out there, and they brought in reinforcements, Jacobs and Thrower could get outnumbered and trapped very easily. At some point, they were going to have to make a move.

Then, they both looked up at the ceiling, hearing

what sounded like the floor creaking above them. Gunner growled even louder, then raced up the stairs to the second floor. Within seconds, they heard the cries of a man screaming.

"I'll take up there!" Jacobs said, racing up the steps to find his partner. As soon as he got up there, he saw Gunner thrashing around, looking like he was trying to take the man's arm off. "Gunner, off!"

Gunner released his grip of the man's arm, who immediately tried to reach for his gun, which had fallen on the floor when Gunner had sunk his teeth into him. Jacobs didn't let him grab it, though, putting two rounds into him.

The front door then broke open, two men rushing inside. Thrower went over to the hallway to greet them, but also heard the back door crash open as well. He went over to the corner of the room where there was an oversized chair and got behind it. Almost immediately, two men from the back showed their faces.

Thrower instantly opened fire, hitting the one in the shoulder. The other retreated behind the wall. Thrower had to duck as the men from the front appeared, firing several rounds into the chair. Gunner came flying down the steps, launching himself on top of one of them, causing them both to fall to the ground with Gunner on top.

The first man tried to help his partner, aiming his gun at Gunner's body. Two shots were fired. The man dropped to his knees with Jacobs looking on after firing the shots. The man then slumped over dead on the floor. The man wrestling with Gunner tried punching him to get the dog off, but he wasn't having much luck. Jacobs finally called Gunner off again so he could deal with him permanently. Once Gunner released his grip, Jacobs put two more rounds into the man.

With his work there done, Gunner then ran through the room Thrower was in, in hopes of finding his next victim. Jacobs and Thrower could both hear that he had. The grunts and growls from Gunner indicated that he had someone's arm in his mouth. Jacobs and Thrower ran into the next room, getting there just in time to see someone else ducking out the back door.

Jacobs called Gunner off the man as he took off running after the man who was getting away. Gunner complied, then ran after his owner. The man still on the ground let out a sigh of relief that he didn't have the dog still on top of him. Thrower had him dead in his sights, though. The man started crawling for his weapon.

"I wouldn't do that," Thrower said, though it appeared his words were falling on deaf ears. The man continued crawling for his gun. "I wouldn't do that."

The man finally reached his weapon and grabbed it. He tried turning around to fire at Thrower, but it was too late. Thrower pulled the trigger one time, ending the man's life.

"I said you shouldn't do that."

Thrower then started walking around the house, making sure no one else was there. He wasn't ready to just accept that was it. And he wasn't letting his guard down. But it did appear that it was over. At least there.

Several minutes later, Jacobs and Gunner came back, walking through the front door. Thrower came over to greet them.

"Did you get him?"

Jacobs shook his head, looking disappointed. "No, he got away."

"Another close call."

Jacobs sighed. "Yeah. Another close call. Seems like a pattern."

They heard the door to the basement open up, with Franks sticking his head out. "Is the coast all clear up here?"

"Yeah."

"Good. I don't like waiting in basements." Franks closed the door once he and Tiffany were out. "They're kind of freaky."

Tiffany went over to Jacobs and gave him a hug. "Are you OK?"

"Yeah, I'm fine."

Franks stood over a couple of the dead bodies. "These guys ain't."

"Definitely not."

"How you supposed they found us here?"

"I dunno. I'm trying to figure that one out too. If it

was your place, maybe they'd have followed you here before or something."

"Yeah, but it ain't. I haven't been here in months."

"And Nate and Tiffany haven't been here, so once again, they're either onto you or me."

"Is it possible they could have followed us from the house?" Tiffany asked.

Jacobs looked at Thrower. "You didn't leave anyone behind, right?"

Thrower shook his head. "No. And nobody followed us either. I kept looking through the back window."

Jacobs threw his arms up, not having an answer. No one actually lived in the house they were in. It was more or less used as a place to bandage people up who didn't want to go to the hospital, or as a temporary hideout if someone needed to lie low for a day or two. Jacobs had been there a few times before when he needed to get fixed up. The four of them kept thinking about how they were found, before Thrower finally spoke up.

"The one constant in all this is you," he said, pointing at Jacobs.

"Me? What do you mean?"

"They lured you out of your house when they attacked there, knowing you wouldn't be there. Then a few minutes after you show up here, they show up too."

"I'm not following."

"Maybe... just maybe... they got you marked."

"Marked?" Franks said. "Whatcha mean, marked?"

"He means they tagged me somehow," Jacobs said.

"But how?"

"That's a good question. How?" Jacobs then looked at Franks, it suddenly hitting him. "The cemetery."

"What? What about it?"

Jacobs didn't explain. He just raced out of the house until he got to his car. The others followed him outside. Jacobs crawled under the car, looking for some kind of GPS or tracking device. Once he got to the rear bumper, he finally found it.

Jacobs got back to his feet and curled his hand into a fist. He then slammed his hand down on the trunk.

"Stupid!"

"What's wrong?" Tiffany asked.

"Because it's me they've been tracking! There's a device right there. I'm so stupid."

"Stop. You're not stupid."

"I can't believe I let them do that!" Jacobs was angry, shaking his head, tapping the car with his hand, and walking around.

"That's what the cemetery meeting was all about," Franks said.

Jacobs nodded. "Yeah. And I was dumb enough to walk right into it. All Ames wanted to do was keep me busy long enough so someone could plant that on my car. And he knew if I had someone there, they'd be focused on him, not the car."

"Pretty smart."

"Yeah, not by me. I let him play me. I can't believe I let it happen."

"What's done is done," Thrower said. "No use beating yourself up over it now."

Jacobs looked at him and nodded. He knew he was right. But he also wished someone would punch him in the face for being so stupid.

"Best be taking that thing off right now," Franks said. "Or else we're gonna get a lot more trouble than we can handle lickety-split."

Jacobs knelt down and was about to take the device off his car, before Thrower stopped him.

"Wait," Thrower said. "Don't do that."

"What?" Jacobs asked. "Why not?"

"Eddie's right."

"He is?"

"I am?" Franks said, surprised.

Jacobs looked just as surprised. "About what?"

"If we don't take that off, we're gonna get a lot more trouble," Thrower said.

"I agree."

"So let's not take it off."

Jacobs stared at Thrower for a moment, then thought he knew what he was saying. He started nodding. Franks looked at the both of them, each of them seemingly knowing what they were talking about without saying a word. He was in the dark, though. He didn't know what was going on.

"Uh, I can see you two are having a, uh, whatever you wanna call it, but I'm still not getting what you're talking about. One of you wanna explain it to me?"

"We can turn a disadvantage into our advantage," Thrower answered.

"How so?"

"They think they've got Brett marked. Let them keep on thinking it. As far as they know, we don't know anything about that device. As far as they're concerned, we must be thinking they followed one of us here. And to his house."

The light looked like it finally came on for Franks. "Ah, I got it now. Ah huh, you sly dog you. I knew I liked you."

"So they've been playing us as fools, so let's turn the tables. Let's make them the fools."

Franks laughed and clapped his hands together. "I like it. I like it."

"We'll take that car somewhere, somewhere we pick, somewhere that we've got a clear advantage, and then let them come."

Jacobs nodded, liking the plan. "And then we'll come down on them like a ton of bricks."

14

F ranks took Tiffany back to his place, while Jacobs and Thrower got themselves ready for what they were sure would be an epic battle. They took separate cars to their destination with Thrower following Jacobs just in case they lost one of them in the fight. With Franks' help in suggesting a location, it took them about twenty-five minutes to get there.

Once they pulled up in front of the small building, they got out and looked around. They were at a manufacturing plant that had gone out of business several years ago. But it would serve their purposes. There was only one way in. The front gate used to be closed tight, but the place had been used by just about every criminal element over the years. Now the gate just stayed open. There wasn't even a lock on it anymore.

The property was also surrounded by tall fences and even taller trees. There were even a couple of older cars near the front gate. One was an old white pickup truck that had clearly seen better days. It looked to be over twenty years old, and one of the tires was flat. In recent years, it was used by kids as a place to smoke.. The other vehicle was a blue van, but that too had fallen on hard times. It didn't even have its front tires anymore. They'd been stolen a long time ago. Now the two vehicles just sat there like statues, greeting people as they came in.

Jacobs and Thrower stood in front of the building and looked at it for a few seconds. Then they walked around a little bit, getting a feel for the area.

"What is this place?" Thrower asked.

"Used to be a manufacturing plant. They made clothes, blankets, fabric, and things like that."

"Ever been here before?"

"Not physically, no. Drove by a few times, but never had to stop in." Jacobs noticed Thrower walking with a slight limp, though he was doing pretty good considering. "Why don't you just sit tight and take it easy? I'll walk around."

"I'm good. Hardly even feel anything. It's just good that it didn't go in too deep or catch the bone."

They walked around the property, getting an idea of where they wanted to set up. Once they were done, they walked back around to the front and stood by their cars, discussing a few ideas.

"I figure we got three options," Jacobs said.

"Probably the same ones I'm thinking of."

"We can wait by the front, out of sight, then surprise them when they come in. Two, we can get inside that building, and mow them down when they get closer. Or three, we can split it. You take one side, I'll take the other. What do you think?"

"Same options I had. But I think there's only one for us. And that's setting up by the entrance."

"Why?"

"If we set up in different spots, there's a chance we could hit each other in the crossfire. That's not very appealing."

Jacobs laughed. "No, it's not."

"From the way it looks, there's only one way out of here, and that's through that gate."

"Yeah."

"Which means if we set up in that building, there's no guarantee we're getting out. They could figure out the same thing and just trap us in there."

"True."

"So I figure we wait by the front, when they come in, we catch them from behind."

Jacobs nodded. He was on board. "Yeah. I agree."

"Might be nice if we had the dog here, just in case. From what I've seen so far, that dog is worth his weight in gold."

"He is. But I feel better knowing that he's with Tiffany. You know, just in case."

"I hear ya. I'd probably do the same."

"At least if he's with her, I know she'll be protected."

"Probably should move my car out of the way, that way when they come in, they only see yours."

Jacobs nodded. "Good idea. Probably best if you take it completely outside, that way if we have to leave in a hurry, we're not blocked by anything."

"How much time you figure until they get here?"

Jacobs shrugged. "I don't know. Seems like they're ramping things up. If they keep that up, shouldn't be long."

Thrower went over to his car and got in. He drove back out of the property, parking the car just down the street. He hobbled back in a few minutes later, finding Jacobs standing there, staring at the building.

"You good?" Thrower asked.

"Yeah. Yeah. Just thinking."

"Anything special?"

"Um, I dunno. Stupid stuff, I guess. Just thinking how peaceful everything seems right now, but in an hour or two there might be dead bodies all over the place."

Thrower nodded. "If we're lucky. And if we're really lucky, we won't be one of them."

"You know, you don't have to do this."

"What?"

"This. Be here. It's not your fight. You were hired to look after Tiffany's parents. This is kind of outside the scope of that agreement, don't you think?"

Thrower shrugged. "I dunno. My nickname's The Bodyguard. A bodyguard's job is to protect people, right? Kind of looks like right now... I'm protecting you."

Jacobs looked at him, then both men laughed. "I hear you. But you still don't have to do this."

"Feels like I'm involved now. Besides, my own personal motto is to try to do what's right. Not necessarily what's best for me. And right now, this is it. Being here feels right."

Jacobs nodded at him. "I appreciate that. I appreciate everything you've done."

"Well, you're paying me, so I guess maybe there's that."

Jacobs smirked. "I have a feeling you'd be here even if I wasn't."

Thrower smiled. "Don't let that get out. I don't want my next jobs to be freebies."

They went over to the vehicles, and Jacobs pulled out his phone. He called Franks, who immediately picked up.

"Hey, what's shaking?"

"Nothing yet," Jacobs replied. "Just wanted to call and make sure everything was good there."

"Oh yeah, man, no worries. We're all good here. We're just sitting here playing cards."

"Cards?"

"Gotta keep busy somehow, you know?"

"I guess so. How's Gunner?"

"He's good. Think he realizes he's missing out on some action though. He seems mopey."

Jacobs laughed. "I'm sure he is. You sure you guys are good?"

"Positive. I made so many turns on the way here I made myself dizzy."

"Should be used to that feeling by now."

"Hey. Anyways, we're all good. I've been checking out the window every couple minutes. The pooch is all quiet, so we're good. No need to worry here."

"OK."

"You just make sure you do what you gotta do on your end."

"We'll do our best."

"Good. There's someone else here that wants to talk to you." Franks handed the phone off to Tiffany. "Brett?"

"Hey."

"Be careful, OK?"

"Always."

"Don't worry about us. We're fine. Just concentrate on you and getting back here in one piece."

"I will."

"That goes for Nate too."

"I'll tell him."

Once Jacobs hung up, he relayed the concerns to his partner. "Tiffany says to make sure you come back in one piece."

Thrower grinned. "I'll do my best."

The two men started setting up, both of them sitting inside the broken-down van. They'd be able to hear any cars coming. While they waited, they passed the time by saying whatever came into their minds.

"She's a nice woman, Tiffany," Thrower said.

"Yeah, she is."

"When I took this job, Eddie told me about your history. Everything you've gone through. I'm glad you're able to turn the corner."

"I'm not gonna lie, it's been a tough road. For a while there, I wasn't sure I was gonna make it. I was about ready to give up."

"What changed?"

"I met Tiffany. I don't know. I met her and... I just started feeling normal again. Like, maybe there was still hope for me."

Thrower smiled. "Amazing what the love of a good woman can do."

"She just accepted me for who I was and believes in me more than I do, probably. I wasn't sure I'd ever find that again. Or if I really deserved it either."

"You do."

"Is this it for you? Hanging up The Eliminator name when this is all over?"

"I dunno. Probably. I was really only doing it to get back at Mallette. And because I was angry. Now I'm just doing it to protect those I care about. Once Ames is gone, I don't think there's anything left for me to really fight for."

"Even when Mallette gets out of prison?"

Jacobs shrugged. "I don't know. I'm torn, you know?

On one hand, I still wanna make him pay. On the other hand, maybe I can have something special with this other woman who believes in me. But I don't know if I can ask her to put that on hold indefinitely while I go fight another battle. I mean, I don't know if it's fair to keep asking her to wait."

Thrower nodded. "You'll make the right call."

"How do you know?"

"Because you'll feel it in your heart. Whichever way you go, you'll know what's right for you."

"What about you? What would you do?"

Thrower shook his head. "I don't know. I can't even imagine. I haven't been through what you've been through. It's different looking at it from the outside. From where I'm looking at it, it's easy. But when you're the one that's had your heart ripped out, it's not so easy."

"What about you? Wife, girlfriend, kids, anything?"

"No. It wouldn't be fair to have someone waiting for me all the time while I travel around the world doing what I do."

"Ever think you might want that?"

"Yeah. Eventually. I'm not gonna be able to do this forever. But I get to travel, see things, and make a lot of money while I'm at it. That way, whenever I do settle down, I'll have a nice cushion to fall back on."

"I take it you're not one of those guys who spends every dollar he's got."

"Not me. I'm socking it all away. When I'm done, I

wanna live on a beach somewhere and pay for the house in cash. No mortgage, don't have to work, just enjoy the sun and the sand."

"Speaking of your work, how'd you get mixed up in this, anyway?"

"Well, I enlisted in the military straight out of high school. My dad was a Marine, so it was just something that seemed to be in the family."

"So why'd you get out?"

Thrower laughed. "Ten years is long enough, don't you think?"

"Yeah, I guess it is."

"I dunno. Just kind of got tired of it. Wanted to do my own thing."

"And your own thing was beating people up for a living?" Jacobs asked with a laugh.

"It's a hard adjustment when you leave the military. You're used to certain things that civilian life just can't provide. And I really didn't have a ton of other options. One day I saw an ad online for a company looking to hire bodyguards. They were protecting politicians and musicians and things like that. Turned out I was pretty good at it. Maybe a little too good. One day I worked some guy over pretty bad who was harassing someone I was protecting. The lawsuit came and there went the job. So I figured since I was pretty good, I'd work for myself. Word got around I was pretty good, and I started taking jobs all over."

"I take it they're not usually mundane and boring assignments?"

"No, I don't usually get those ones. Ain't nobody hiring me to keep teenagers away from a pop star or something. I usually get hired when someone's life has been threatened, and their own security team either isn't enough or isn't qualified enough to handle it."

"Well, you're certainly good at it. No doubt about that."

"You're not too bad yourself. After this is over, you should think about training dogs or something. You've done a good job with yours."

Jacobs smiled. "I wish I could take all the credit for it. I taught him some things, worked with him, but sometimes... sometimes I feel like he trained himself, you know? He's one smart dog."

"I can tell. I might have you train one for me that I can take wherever I go."

"Hey, you find the dog, and I might take you up on that."

They laughed for a few seconds, but the good times were quickly silenced when they heard the sound of car engines nearby. They looked over the front seats, through the windshield, and saw a bunch of cars going past them.

"Here they are," Thrower said.

"You ready for this?"

Thrower nodded. "Let's show them who's boss."

15

Ten cars passed them. Jacobs and Thrower weren't going to reveal themselves until they knew for sure that was all they were dealing with. They waited an extra minute or two. They looked out the window of the van, seeing Ames' men pile out of their vehicles. There appeared to be between twenty and thirty men milling around the front of the building. Once again, it didn't look like Ames was among them.

"Follow my lead?" Jacobs asked.

"Right behind you."

Jacobs snuck out the back door of the van and went around to the front of it, using the vehicle as a shield. Thrower did the same, but went to the back. Jacobs was the first to open up, firing his rifle. Thrower started firing as soon as he heard the first shot.

Chaos ensued as Ames' men started hitting the ground. With several men dead already, the rest of them started to disperse. Some got behind their cars, and some got into the building. They all tried to figure out where the shots were coming from. It only took a few seconds before they figured it out. Then they started to return fire.

Both sides were locked into their positions for the next several minutes as the bullets went back and forth. For Jacobs and Thrower, the idea wasn't to stay there all day and engage in a battle. They simply wanted to dwindle the numbers of Ames' crew a little more. They'd already accomplished that.

And while they would have liked to take more out, they also knew that reinforcements might have already been on the way. They couldn't stay and get outnumbered in an overwhelming fashion. They had to hit and move. Keep Ames' crew on the defensive. Keep them guessing as to where they'd show up next.

"Another minute and let's split!" Jacobs yelled to his partner.

"Got it!"

Both men continued firing, trying to pick off a few more men before they left the scene. Before leaving, each of them mowed down two more men. Thrower left his position and joined up with Jacobs at the hood of the car.

"Why don't you grab the car first and I'll cover you?" Jacobs said. "Then bring it up to the gate."

"Right." Thrower gave it about three seconds, then tapped Jacobs on the shoulder to let him know he was going. He raised himself up and ran towards the gate.

To keep his partner covered, Jacobs fired at a furious pace, not aiming for anyone in particular, but wanting to keep Ames' men ducking for cover so they didn't have a target to shoot at. He quickly looked back and saw that Thrower had made it through the gate.

While he waited, Jacobs took aim again, hitting one more man before he heard the wheels of Thrower's car speeding up near the gate. Jacobs looked back and saw the car, then took off running as fast as he could. Thrower had the back door open for him, so by the time Jacobs got there, he had to just dive in. As soon as he was in, Thrower hit the gas, speeding off as fast as possible.

"Looks like that was a success," Thrower said.

"Yeah, we took out a few of them."

"How many you think we hit?"

"I dunno. Maybe ten?"

"It's a solid number. Chopping them down a little at a time. Keep doing enough of that, and pretty soon Ames will have to start doing his own dirty work."

Jacobs laughed. "I'm not sure about that. But we can hope."

Once the pair got back to Franks' place and walked through the door, Tiffany ran over to Jacobs and hugged him.

"Everything's fine," Jacobs said, putting his arms around her.

"I know I said I wouldn't do this, but I worry every time you walk out that door."

Jacobs knew there was nothing he could really say that would ease her mind. "I know. Just know that I'm doing everything I can to be as safe as possible."

Franks came walking over. He looked at Thrower. "I like you and all, but if you think I'm hugging you, you got another thing coming."

Thrower laughed. "I'll take a high-five instead."

"Well, that I can give you. So how'd everything go out there?"

"About as well as expected," Jacobs said. "Took out about ten of them."

Franks clapped his hands together. "Now that's what I'm talking about. Bringing them numbers down."

Jacobs didn't seem as enthused as his friend. "Yeah, but we're not gonna be able to keep doing that."

"Why not?"

"For one, they're not gonna fall for that again. By now, they've gotta realize we know about the tracker on the car, and that we lured them there. Two, they're gonna be on their guard for anything from here on out."

"Doesn't hurt to try."

"And three, I need another new car. Had to leave the other one there, and I'm not going back for it now."

"Another new car?!" Franks said. "Man, how many cars are you gonna go through? You go through cars like some people go through cheeseburgers. You just eat them right up." Jacobs smiled and shrugged. He didn't have any response. "So now I gotta find you a car and a new place to live?"

"That's the business you're in, isn't it?"

"Man, I need to raise my prices for all the extra work I'm doing."

"Speaking of houses, how's that working out?"

"I'm working on it, I'm working on it. Already got some feelers out."

Thrower stood there silently, letting the others converse with themselves, while he contemplated things from Ames' point of view. He tried to put himself in his shoes. And he wasn't liking what he came up with.

"I hate to be a wet blanket, but I think I should go," Thrower said.

"What, where you going?" Franks asked.

"I still have the Vogels to look after."

"I told you, I got that."

"Yeah, I know, but right now, they're my responsibility."

"Nate, what's wrong?" Tiffany asked, getting the sense that he knew something he wasn't sharing.

Thrower cleared his throat. "After what just happened, I just think I should be there."

"You think they're gonna try something?" Jacobs asked.

"Well, I'm trying to put myself in Ames' position.

I'm amping up the pressure. I broke into your place and tried to take out Tiffany. Lost a few men there. Followed you to the safe house and tried again to take you out. Lost a few more men there. Then I get lured to that warehouse and lose a bunch more men there. Now I'm angry. I'm really pissed. None of my plans are working, I'm losing men left and right, everything's failing. So what do I do?"

"Leave town?" Franks said.

"No. I've got two options. I either recoil and go hide somewhere for a while, regroup, try for another time."

"Or I keep trying to hit, figuring eventually I'll break through," Jacobs said, anticipating Thrower's thoughts.

Thrower nodded. "And since I've lost the tracker, and I have no idea where any of us are, there's one more thing I can do right now. There is someone I do know that will make you hurt."

"Tiffany's parents."

Thrower nodded again.

"But they've already tried that," Tiffany said.

"If they're going to stay on the offensive, it's the only move they've got right now," Thrower said.

"Well, maybe they'll just realize they're not winning and go away for a while."

Thrower shrugged. "It's always possible. I just wanna err on the side of caution. I think I should be there in case."

"If you're going, I should go with you," Jacobs said.

"Let's go."

"I wanna go too," Tiffany said.

Jacobs turned to face her and put his hands on her shoulders. "No. It's too dangerous. You've already been through a lot. Stay here with Eddie." Jacobs heard Gunner whining and looked down at him. "You too, buddy. Stay here and protect them." Jacobs then looked at Franks. "You keep working on that house and car."

Franks nodded. "I'll take care of it."

Thrower had already left the house to get the car warmed up. Jacobs ran out the door.

Just as he exited, Tiffany spoke up. "Let me know if they're OK!" She wasn't sure if Jacobs heard her.

Franks gently squeezed her arm to comfort her. "They'll make sure your parents are OK. Don't worry about that."

Tiffany looked at him and faked a smile. Her eyes were getting glossy. "I don't understand why. Why all this is happening. Why are people so cruel and heartless?"

Franks shook his head, not really having a good reason. "I don't know, honey. It's just the way of the world, I guess. It's cold, ruthless, and unforgiving at times. Thankfully, there are also good people in it who are willing to stop people like that. Don't you worry, though. If there's anything to be stopped, those two will stop it."

~

Jacobs and Thrower pulled onto the Vogels' street. Almost immediately, they knew something was wrong. They slowly drove past the house, looking at each car that was parked along the curb. There was no one in any of them.

"Where are the guards?" Thrower asked.

"I don't know. That's a good question."

"There's supposed to be two of them, right?"

"That's what Eddie said."

Thrower drove down the street, then turned around and went back the way they came to make sure they didn't miss anything.

"Still not seeing anything," Jacobs said.

Thrower looked at the Vogels' house, seeing one of their cars was missing. He parked along the curb across from the house, then tapped Jacobs on the arm and pointed at the driveway. "His car is missing."

"So did just Mr. Vogel go somewhere, and she's still here, or did they go somewhere together?"

"With two guards, if they split up, I'd think one of them would have stayed here," Thrower said.

Jacobs immediately got out his phone and called Franks. "Eddie. The guards aren't here."

"Then where are they?"

"I don't know. I want you to call them and find out where they are and what's happening. Mr. Vogel's car is missing, so they might have followed him somewhere. I just wanna make sure."

"All right, give me a minute to check. I'll call you back."

While they waited for Franks to call back, Jacobs and Thrower kept their eyes glued to the house in case they saw Mrs. Vogel.

Franks tried calling the number to one of the guards, but got no response. He then tried calling the other one, but still no answer. He thought it was a little strange, but wasn't ready to panic yet. Once he tried each of the numbers again, still with neither of them picking up, he then started to worry.

Tiffany was at the kitchen table, watching Franks try to get a hold of someone. He didn't tell her what he was doing, not wanting to make her even more anxious and nervous than she already was. But she could see that something wasn't right.

"What's the matter?" Tiffany asked.

"Oh, it's, uh, nothing. Nothing at all." Franks let out an uncomfortable smile. "Just trying to get you guys a new place. Not always easy bargaining things like this."

Tiffany nodded but wasn't totally buying what Franks was trying to sell her. She had a feeling it had something to do with her parents. By the look on Franks' face, it seemed like he was worried about something. In the short time she'd known him, she didn't think he'd worry much about finding a house.

Franks kept trying the numbers of the two guards

for a few more minutes. He even tried sending them text messages, hoping they'd respond in some way. But they were still silent. He looked at his phone, not sure what to do next. He glanced over at Tiffany, trying to remain calm so as not to give anything away and make her more concerned than she already was.

Franks dialed Jacobs back, glancing over at Tiffany, and choosing his words carefully. "Uh, yeah, that's, uh, that's a no-go on that request."

"What?"

"I, uh, can't really divulge anything further. But in regard to your conditions, I cannot meet them."

"Are you trying to talk in code?"

"That's right."

"Tiffany's nearby?"

"Right again."

Jacobs sighed, knowing what he was saying. "You can't reach the guys?"

"No, I cannot."

"Damn. What are we gonna do now?"

"Uh, I don't know. We could always ask the subject who knows them best to see if they can reach out to them and see if they get a response, but that would involve someone getting clued in on that."

"Hold on." Jacobs took the phone away from his ear and let Thrower know. "What do you think?"

"Well, if there's something wrong, she's gonna find out about it sooner or later anyway. And if there is, the sooner we can get on it, the better off they'll be. If we wait a while, and they are in trouble, it might be too late to save them."

Jacobs agreed, putting the phone back to his ear. "Have Tiffany call them."

"You sure?" Franks asked.

"Yeah. If there's a problem, the sooner we know, the better we'll be."

"OK. I'll let you know how it goes."

Franks walked over to Tiffany. She was staring at him the whole time. By the way he was walking and the look on his face, she immediately thought there was trouble.

"There's something wrong, isn't there? I can tell."

Franks put his hands out. "Now, now, there's nothing to get alarmed about yet."

"Yet? There is something wrong."

"Just relax. We don't know if there's a problem yet. Right now, we don't know where the guards are. They're not outside your parents' house, and they're not responding to my calls or texts."

"Oh my god."

"Just wait, just wait. Your dad's car is missing. Now, that doesn't mean they're in trouble. Could be they went somewhere, the guards followed, and they can't get a signal or something. Do you know where your parents might be?"

Tiffany put her hands on her head. "Uh, I'm not sure. They like to be outdoors a lot. Go to parks, trails, go down by the lakes, fish. They could be anywhere."

"Do you wanna try to get them on the phone? If they answer, don't indicate anything is wrong. Just say you're calling just to say hi. And see if you can find out where they are."

"And if they don't pick up?"

"They'll pick up." Franks wasn't sure if he believed that, but he had to keep Tiffany's mind at ease as much as possible. "They'll pick up."

Tiffany immediately called her mom. Her nerves frayed after each ring. Finally, on the fifth ring, her mom answered.

"Mom?" Tiffany was happy she answered, but almost shocked at the same time. She had just about convinced herself that something was wrong.

"Hi, Tiff, how are you?"

"I'm fine. Are you OK?"

"Yeah, we're fine, why? Is something wrong?"

"Uh, no, no. I, uh, just drove by the house and saw that you weren't there."

"Oh, you should've let us know you were coming."

"So where'd you guys go?" Tiffany asked.

"We're down by the lake. Your dad is fishing and I'm just reading a book."

"Oh. OK."

"You can always come down and join us if you want. We'll probably be here a few more hours or so."

"Oh, thanks, but I don't think I can. I was going to see Brett soon."

"Oh, that's nice. He seems like a nice guy. We can't wait to see him again."

"Yeah, maybe soon we can all get together again," Tiffany replied.

"Definitely."

"OK, well, I'm going to call Brett now. I'll talk to you soon, Mom, OK?"

"Love you, dear."

"Love you too," Tiffany said.

Tiffany put the phone down, looking and sounding relieved. "They're at the lake. She said they're fine."

Franks looked a little surprised. "Oh. Well... that's good." He was actually expecting a different result. But he was happy to hear it anyhow. He got back on his phone and immediately called Jacobs.

"Yeah?" Jacobs answered, also expecting the worst.

"They're fine."

"What?"

"Tiffany just talked to her mom. They're down by the lake. They'll be there a few more hours."

Jacobs breathed a little easier. "Well, that's a relief. What about those guards, though?"

"Yeah, I don't know. I'll keep trying."

In the middle of their conversation, Jacobs' phone started buzzing. There was another call coming in. He looked at the number and immediately knew it was bad news. "I'll call you back, Eddie. Ames is calling."

"Ames is calling?"

Jacobs hung up on Franks, then answered Ames' call. "What do you want?"

Ames let out a laugh. "I've gotta hand it to you. You're a very resourceful guy. Seems no matter what kind of shit I throw against the wall, it just doesn't stick."

"Sorry to hear it. Better luck next time."

"Luring us to that warehouse was a nice touch," Ames said.

"Well, you went through all the trouble of putting that tracker underneath my car, I didn't want it to go to waste."

"I almost had you."

"Almost. If you wanna meet me right now, I can give you your runners-up prize."

"Oh, we'll be meeting soon enough."

"Just so you know, when it comes time to kill you, I'm gonna make sure it hurts extra special," Jacobs said.

"You're getting too personal. Tiffany did nothing to you."

"She knows you. That's enough."

"And I thought Mallette was bad enough. You might be even worse."

Ames laughed. "I'll take that as a complement. Be that as it may, we have other business to discuss here."

"And what's that?"

"If you've been trying to check in with those guards you have on the Vogels' house, you may be wondering where they are just about now."

"What did you do?"

"Well, right now they're safe and sound, but only for the moment. If you don't agree to my terms, they'll be dead within the hour."

"What are your terms?"

"Before we get to that, also know that my men have eyes on the Vogels as we speak. In case you don't know where they are, the lake is lovely this time of year. So if you choose to believe that the guards are expendable, and believe me, if I were in your shoes, I'd let them perish. But aside from that, I have a very accomplished shooter with a rifle scope planted firmly on the back of the head of Tiffany's mother. She's sitting alone reading a book right now. If you'd like, we can put her head in the story, if you catch my meaning."

"You're one evil..."

"Now, now, before you start cursing me all over the place, perhaps you'd like to hear my terms on how to keep them alive and healthy?"

"I'm listening."

"I want you to meet me in one hour at a place of my choosing. Once you arrive, I'll call my men off the parents and release your guards."

"What guarantee do I have?"

"Well, I guess you don't really have one. But, if you do nothing, they're as good as dead anyway, so you might as well take the chance. But all I really want is you. They're basically just a way to get to you. If I have you, they're not really needed anymore. And I doubt

Tiffany or her parents could hurt me after you're gone."

"You'll let them go."

"If you agree to my terms, then yes. I'll leave them alone after this. On one condition."

"What's that?"

"You bring that new guy with you. He's becoming irritating as well."

"Can't. He's dead."

"Oh, come now, do you really expect me to believe that?"

"It's true."

"I know very well he was the one who saved Tiffany inside your place. And I know he was at the warehouse when you ambushed my men. So don't go giving me some sob story."

"It's not a story. He took a knife when saving Tiffany. We were able to fix him up, but he took a couple bullets at the warehouse as we were leaving. Eddie took him to a hospital, but he didn't make it. He died before he got there."

"I should be so angry that I take out her mother right now just for you having the stones to think I'm so gullible to believe that."

"It's not a story. It's true. He's dead. I'm sorry I didn't take a picture for you, but he's gone. I can't bring someone with me who's not even breathing."

"OK. Let's just say I'll take your word for it for now. Who is the guy, anyway?"

"Couldn't tell you. Eddie hired him. He was just a bodyguard to me. Only thing I knew about him was his name was Andy. Never got a last name."

"Fine, I'll go with that for now. You're the main thing I want, anyway."

"So what's the deal?" Jacobs asked.

"Simple. You come to the place I tell you. Bring that dog of yours with you. Then when I see you, I'll tell my men to stand down on the Vogels. That's the deal."

"What do you want the dog for?"

"He's almost as much of a pain in the ass as you are. And I don't wanna take the chance of dealing with him again after this. So that's the deal. Do you want to show? Or do you wanna be the one to break it to your girlfriend that you let her parents die, and you did nothing about it?"

"I'll show up. Just tell me where."

16

Jacobs and Thrower went back to Franks' place so they could grab Gunner, since he was needed for part of the deal. When they got there, Tiffany greeted Jacobs with a hug like she usually did. She had no idea what was about to come down since Jacobs didn't let anyone else know before he got there.

"So what'd Ames want?" Franks asked.

Tiffany looked back at him, confused, then turned toward Jacobs again. "Ames? What? What's going on?"

Jacobs glared at Franks for a second, a little peeved that he let the cat out of the bag already, though he supposed he wasn't going to be able to keep the secret from Tiffany, anyway.

Jacobs cleared his throat. "Uh, Ames called after you talked to your mom."

"And? Are they OK?" Tiffany was starting to get worried all over again.

"Um, Ames kidnapped their guards. He knows where your parents are."

"Oh my god, we have to go get them."

Jacobs shook his head. "There isn't time."

"What? What are you saying? You're just gonna let them..."

Jacobs put his hands on Tiffany's shoulders to calm her down. "No. No. They're gonna be fine. I'm who he wants."

Tiffany scrunched her face together the way someone did when they were battling a glare from the sun, and shook her head, not quite sure what he was trying to say. "What do you mean? What's going on?"

"I'm supposed to meet Ames in about an hour with Gunner. Once he sees me, he'll call off whoever's on your parents."

Tiffany stared at him for a few moments, letting it sink in. "Soooo, you're just, what? Gonna give yourself up to him? Is that what you're saying?"

"That's what he wants."

"And you're just gonna do it? Just like that? You're gonna trade your life for theirs? Because we all know he's gonna kill you if you do that."

Jacobs shrugged. "What other choice is there?"

"We fight," Franks answered. "That's the other choice. We don't just go hiding in a closet when the mice come in. We fight them head on, man. We lick those suckers."

Jacobs knew what he was saying, though, like

usual, it was a terrible choice of metaphors. He looked away for a second. "Well…"

"There's no wells, man. He wants you and Gunner, so we'll give him you and Gunner."

Jacobs, Tiffany, and Thrower all looked at Franks, unsure at what he was getting at.

Franks looked at each of them. "And a whole lot more! That's what I'm getting at!"

"Ames is likely going to have everyone he's got left there," Jacobs said. "Could be twenty, thirty, forty men still."

"So?"

"I mean, we're good, but he's not gonna release the order on Tiff's parents until he sees we're there and not giving a problem."

"So we make him think you're not giving a problem."

Jacobs sighed. "Listen, I know you're just trying to help, but maybe it's just time. Maybe this is as far as I can go."

Tiffany lunged at Jacobs and hugged him close. "Don't ever say that."

"Besides, it's not just you and Gunner going," Thrower said. "You can count me in."

Jacobs looked at him and instantly shook his head. "No. No, I appreciate the gesture, but I can't. You can't."

Thrower grinned. "Pretty sure that's my call."

"You know what you'll be walking into."

Thrower's smile widened. "I got nowhere else to be."

"Nate, look, I can't..."

"It's already settled. I'm going. That's my call."

"I'm going too," Franks said.

"What?" Jacobs said. "What do you plan on doing?"

"Hey, I dunno, I'll figure it out. I always do."

"You and guns don't exactly go together."

"Hey, I saved you from, uh, uh, uh, what's her name?"

"Yeah, and I still say that was a lucky shot."

"Got the job done, didn't I?"

"I'll go too," Tiffany said.

Jacobs put his hands up. "Whoa, whoa, whoa. Let's just pump the brakes here a little bit. If Nate wants to come, fine, I know he can handle himself. If Eddie wants to come, I guess I'll OK it. But in no way, absolutely no way, are you coming. That is a capital NO."

"But..."

"No buts. You've never even fired a gun, and I wouldn't even dream of putting you in that kind of situation. I'd be too worried about you to worry about what I was doing. No. You're not going. But I appreciate the thought."

"I got an idea," Franks said, a smirk forming on his face.

"What's that?"

"You've still got a friend on the police force, right?"

Jacobs instantly shook his head, thinking he knew

what was coming. "No, won't work. If I tell Bucky and they swoop in on Ames, he might have given orders to his guys that if they don't hear from him, that they take out her parents automatically. Can't chance that."

"That's not what I'm thinking."

"Then what?"

"Tiffany finds out exactly where her parents are. She goes down to meet them. We have Buchanan meet her there too, with maybe a few extra officers. Let them feel the police presence there."

"Doesn't mean they won't take a shot."

"Hear me out, man. You go meet Ames as agreed. When he sees you, you make sure you don't do anything until he tells his guys to stand down. Then when he does, you give me a signal. Scratch behind your ear or something. When I see that, I'll call Tiff and let her know. Then she and Buchanan can take her parents away to safety. What do you think?"

"A lot of moving parts."

"Could work, though," Thrower said.

"Yeah. Maybe," Jacobs said.

"But we ain't got time to dilly-dally," Franks said.

"If we start fighting, though, what's to prevent Ames from putting the order back on again?" Jacobs asked.

"If the cops get them to safety, it'll be too late for them to do anything."

"I got a better idea," Thrower said.

"What's that, my man?"

"We can still do Eddie's plan. But I keep a rifle pointed at Ames. As soon as I see that signal from Brett, I take him out. That way when things go down, he's not able to give the order. And the rest of them will be too busy ducking bullets to care at that point."

Franks nodded and smiled. "I like it. I like it."

"What do you think?" Thrower asked Jacobs.

Jacobs thought about it. "It could work."

"It's our best shot," Franks said. "Ain't no captain going down with the ship on my watch. This ain't the Titanic. Ain't no iceberg taking this boat down. We're all making it to shore."

"If we're gonna do it, we need to get things in motion now," Thrower said. "Time's ticking."

"Everyone agree it's the best plan?" Jacobs asked, looking at each of them. They all agreed that it was. "OK." He got out his phone and called Buchanan, hoping he wasn't already at a crime scene or in the middle of an investigation that he couldn't pull himself away from.

Thankfully, Buchanan picked up immediately. "What's up, Brett?"

"I need a favor from you. I don't have a lot of time to go into it, and it's gonna take you trusting me, but I could really use your help."

"Name it."

"I need you to grab a couple of uniformed guys and head down to Rainbow Beach."

"What for?"

"Protection. Two people there are in danger."

"Names, faces?"

"I'm gonna text you the phone number of a girl named Tiffany. She's gonna meet you there. She's their daughter. When you get there, call her so she sees you. She'll explain everything."

"This Tiffany... is she a flake or something?"

"She's... special to me. I need this."

"Part of your healing process?"

"Something like that."

"Say no more. Just tell me one thing."

"What's that?"

"This Tiffany... is she gonna help you get back to the old you?"

"I think so."

"That's good enough for me. I'll be there."

"Thanks, Bucky. I owe you. More than I can ever probably repay."

"Hey, if you and this girl... you make this work... that's all the payment I'll ever need."

"Thank you."

"I'll get there in about fifteen minutes."

Jacobs put his phone back in his pocket, then looked at Tiffany. "You should probably get going so you can meet him there. He said he'll get there in fifteen minutes."

Tiffany still looked worried. "What about you?"

Jacobs grinned, trying to put her mind at ease a

little. "Hey, with all these guys behind me, how could we go wrong?"

Tiffany's eyes started tearing up. She put her arms around him and pulled him tight to her body. "Please come back to me."

Jacobs took a second to actually enjoy holding her. He put his face into the side of her hair. It was a moment that he didn't want to give up. "I'll do everything I can."

Tiffany reluctantly pulled away. She got down on one knee in front of Gunner and started petting him. "You make sure you bring him back to me, OK?" Gunner let out a growl. "You better come back to me too, understand?" Gunner then licked her face. Tiffany wiped her eyes, then stood back up and looked at the rest of the team. "You all be careful, OK?"

"Don't worry," Thrower said. "I'll make sure everyone gets back."

"I'll hold you to that."

"You better get going," Jacobs said.

"I know you've talked about Buchanan before, but..."

"You can trust him. I wouldn't trust anyone else for this."

"OK." Tiffany leaned into him and planted a kiss on his lips. "Let me know when you're safe."

"I will."

They all stood there and watched Tiffany walk out the door. Franks and Thrower left the room to get themselves ready and armed, while Jacobs went over to the window. He watched Tiffany as she walked to her car. Just before she got in, she looked back and saw Jacobs standing at the window. She gave him a little wave, a gesture that Jacobs returned. She got in her car and drove off.

Jacobs stood there at the window, not wanting to move, watching until Tiffany's car was out of sight. Thrower came over to him and put his hand on Jacobs' shoulder.

"Don't worry. You'll see her again."

"I sure hope so," Jacobs said. "I'd like to think…" He never finished his thought, but Thrower knew where he was going with it.

"C'mon, let's get ready. We do this right, you'll be on the beach with her sipping some fruity drinks in no time."

Jacobs grinned. "Yeah." Though he certainly appreciated the words of encouragement, his friends were a little more confident in how things would play out than he was. He was hopeful, but his mind kept going to a dark place. He sure would have hated if this was the end for him. Just as he thought his life was going in a new direction, with a woman that he cared about. Now that there was light at the end of the tunnel, he sure hoped there wasn't a train coming.

17

Jacobs, Franks, and Thrower put everything they thought they'd need into the car. Guns, ammo, any equipment they even thought had a chance of being used, it was there. And they all had bullet-proof vests on.

"How do you guys even move with these things on," Franks said, squirming around to make it fit better. "So uncomfortable, man."

"You get used to it," Jacobs said.

Thrower tapped Franks on the back, making him stumble forward a bit. "Yeah, after a while, you don't even feel the weight anymore."

Franks just looked at him. "You don't say?"

"Might as well get this show on the road," Jacobs said.

Franks looked at the time. "What's the hurry? We still got a little time."

"Let's just do this and get it over with. The sooner Tiffany's parents are out of trouble, the better I'll feel. Plus, you guys will need a few extra minutes to get into a good position."

"Speaking of that," Thrower said. "What kind of layout are we looking at here?"

"I don't know. I've never been there."

"I have," Franks said, scratching his cheek. "It's been a while, but it's a secluded spot. There are two or three buildings there. There's the main one in the middle, a bigger one, then two smaller buildings, one on each side."

"How many floors?"

"Each one is two."

"Entrances? Exits?"

Franks grabbed a piece of paper from the car and went over to the hood. The others followed him. He started drawing the layout of the area as best he could. "Don't know about exits. All I know is the one in front. Whether there's another one in back, I can't say. Didn't go back that far."

"What kind of buildings are they?" Thrower asked.

"I don't know. I think the two smaller ones on the side were office buildings or something, and the one in the middle was for manufacturing or warehousing or something like that. I'm not sure. Never really asked."

"What about us? We can't go in the front door. I assume there's a fence around the property?"

"Oh yeah, you can count on that. Probably about six or eight feet, something like that."

"Well, if there's a back entrance, you can assume Ames will probably have a guard on it," Jacobs said.

"No doubt, man."

"Which once again leaves the question," Thrower said. "How are we getting in? If I'm gonna take out Ames as soon as you give your signal, I'm gonna need a clear line of sight right to him."

"What about nearby buildings?" Jacobs asked.

"You think this is Ames' first rodeo?" Franks said. "You think he's gonna hold this little shindig in downtown Chicago? No!"

"Let me guess, it's a secluded area."

"Well, I mean, it ain't in Timbuktu or nothing, but as I recall, there wasn't much around it. Certainly not another building Nate's gonna be able to use."

"Still the same question, then," Thrower said. "We've gotta be able to get in unseen, or else this isn't gonna work. If I have to fight my way in, that's gonna throw the whole plan off. And if that's the case, we might as well just both plow through the front in a tank."

Jacobs thought about it for a few seconds. "How close are these buildings to each other and the perimeter?"

Franks rubbed his chin. "As I recall, the two end buildings were slanted in a little, like facing the one in the middle. Not all the way, just a slight angle."

"How much distance between the end buildings and the fence?"

Franks shrugged. "Can't say exactly. It's been a few years. But as I recall, it's not too far."

"Could you see the back of the building from the front?"

"No, not too much."

Jacobs looked at Thrower. "Guess there's your answer. You're gonna have to cut your way in and get to that back of one of those buildings."

Thrower pointed to one of the side buildings. "If I get through the fence over here, and make my way to the back of the building, I'll have to try to get into the building and make my way up to the second floor."

"Might be tough if Ames has got people stationed in back."

"Yeah. I don't see another way, though."

"What if he's already got men stationed inside that building?" Franks asked.

Thrower started shaking his head. "I'll just have to take out whoever's in my way. Quietly."

"Yeah," Jacobs agreed. "Because if you get into a loud battle before I show up, everything's out the window. Pressure's gonna be on you."

Thrower cleared his throat. "Yeah." He looked at the other two men, knowing all the pressure would be on him to sneak in quietly. He already knew that was going to be a tall order. But it was one that he needed to fulfill.

"Where you want me to be?" Franks asked.

"Right behind him."

"You don't want me in that other building?"

"No."

"Why?"

"Because you're not a fighter, Eddie. If Ames has men outside or inside that building, I don't have confidence that you're fighting your way in quietly."

"Gee, thanks a lot."

"Hey, we all have our skill sets. This isn't at the top of your list. If you're behind Nate, you'll be there to support him and make sure nobody comes up on his rear. Or if he's engaged, you can be his eyes. It's still an important job."

"All right, man, all right. Hey, Tiffany and Buchanan should be at the beach by now, right?" Franks asked.

Jacobs nodded. "Yeah."

"Why not just have them grab the parents now and whisk them to safety? Why wait for our signal?"

"Because police presence or not, what makes you think they won't shoot them with the cops around? Maybe they have orders to shoot if anyone makes a move to try to escort them from the area."

"Oh. Yeah. Didn't think of that."

"Are you willing to take that risk?"

"Not me, man."

"We'll wait for the signal. I want them to hear

Ames' voice telling them to stand down. Anything else is a gamble I don't want to take."

With everything squared away, they hopped in the car and drove to the meeting spot. They pulled off the main road, driving onto a small side road that led through a group of trees on both sides of the road. They still couldn't see the buildings yet, though there was a brief outline of the fence that could be seen from that position.

"Let us out here," Thrower said as they reached the first line of trees. "We'll use the trees to get us in there without being spotted. They might have lookouts further up."

"OK. Got your comms in?"

Thrower put his in his ear. "We're good."

"I'm good," Franks said.

Jacobs looked at the time. "Still got about fifteen minutes. That enough time for you?"

"I'll make it work," Thrower said.

"Just give me all the time that you can. Stall if you have to."

"I'll do what I can. Just let me know when you're in position."

"You got it," Jacobs said.

Thrower and Franks, with backpacks on, got out of the car and immediately started running through the trees toward the side of the property. Jacobs watched them move until they were no longer visible. He checked the time again. He was going to give them every possible second that they needed.

Jacobs looked over at Gunner, who was sitting in the passenger seat. He smiled at him and rubbed his head.

"You ready for this, buddy?"

Gunner let out a low-sounding growl, and lowered his head, indicating he liked being pet in that spot. Once Jacobs stopped, Gunner barked at him.

"Yeah, I hope we make it out of this too."

Gunner then let out a strange mix that sounded like a cross between a bark and a growl.

"I don't know. Maybe. Hey, if I don't make it and you do, I want you to... well, I was gonna say stick with Eddie, but you love Tiff too, so I don't know, pick whoever you want, I guess."

Gunner barked at him again.

"Yeah, I know, I shouldn't talk like that. But I just want you to be prepared in case."

Jacobs continued talking to Gunner for the rest of the time that Thrower needed to get around to the side. It helped to pass the time. It also helped him to not think about all the bad things that could happen in the next few minutes.

Knowing what could happen, Jacobs' mind then went to his family. The past couple years, he'd always been so willing to join them. He'd always gone into any battle completely at ease with the prospect of not making it out. Now, it was strange. Now, he wasn't ready.

His thoughts went to Tiffany, and how he knew she was what he needed to get back to a good place. She was kind, patient, loving, and caring. And he wasn't ready to lose that too.

After the fifteen minutes was up, Jacobs knew he had to get moving. But he still wanted to give Thrower as much time as possible.

"Nate, how you making out?"

"Cutting through the gate now."

"How's it looking once you get past it?"

Thrower looked through the fence. He saw two men standing near the back door of the building he needed to get to. "Looks like I'm gonna have my work cut out for me."

"It's not a clear path?"

"No, it's not."

"I'll give you as much time as I can."

"Don't worry. I'll get there."

As Jacobs started slowly driving on the road again, Thrower continued looking through the fence, checking to see if there were any more men he'd have to deal with besides the two obvious ones. He didn't see anyone, though that didn't mean there weren't any lurking around somewhere. But for right now, his focus was on the two at the back door.

"How are we gonna handle that?" Franks asked.

"I don't know. But we need to be quick about it."

"I could always go in first, try to draw their attention to me. Then you sneak up behind them."

"What makes you think they won't shoot first?"

"Oh. Yeah. Good thought. Nix that."

"Or that you'll be able to turn their backs to me."

"You got something else in mind?"

Thrower looked up and down the fence, trying to see if there was a better spot he could go in at. He looked at the fence in relation to the building and thought he had something. He continued cutting through the fence in the spot they were.

"Here, you go in here." Thrower then pointed farther up the fence. "I'm gonna go up that way and get in through there."

"What do you want me to do?"

"Just go in."

"And stand there?"

"Yeah."

"What about that shooting thing?"

"All you need to do is move them a few steps towards you. Then I can get in behind them over there."

"Without a sound?"

"That's the plan."

"Man, I hope you know what you're doing. Or we're all gonna be up the creek without a paddle."

"I told Brett we're gonna get there, and we will. Or we're all going down together."

18

Thrower held the fence steady with his free hand as he clipped the last remaining section of the fence. He was trying to be as quiet as possible so as not to alert anyone he was there. Once the section was removed, he took his backpack off and shoved that through the new hole first. He then slid in on his stomach. He was on the side of the building, but there were a bunch of bushes there, preventing him from being seen by anyone in the front.

He quickly got up on one knee and took two knives out, holding one in each hand. He waited patiently until Franks did his part, which he hoped wouldn't take too long. They couldn't afford to wait. Luckily, he then saw Franks' head getting through the fence.

"Hey," one of the guards said, pointing at Franks' position.

Franks just stood there, not saying a word. He simply put his hands up high over his head to signify he wasn't a threat.

Thrower waited a couple seconds, not wanting to move until he saw the outline of the first man appear. Then he saw it. And he wasted no time in getting to him. Thrower raced over to the man, jumping onto his back, twisting the knife from his left hand into the man's side as they fell to the ground.

As soon as they hit the ground, Thrower's attention immediately went to the other man at the door. The remaining guard seemed in shock at what was happening, though he didn't have long to look at it. Just as Thrower hit the ground, while keeping the knife in his man's side, with his right hand, he threw the other knife at the remaining guard. It hit its mark, lodging into the man's chest. The guard dropped to his knees.

Wanting to make sure everything remained quiet, Thrower couldn't afford to have the guard yell out in pain. He took out the knife from the guard's side, then threw it at the guard by the door. The second knife drove into the man's stomach, causing him to finally fall over onto the ground.

Thrower looked around to make sure no one else was there. They were all clear. He waved at Franks to come over to him. Franks immediately ran in his direction, both of them getting to the back door. Thrower pulled his knives out of the dead man, then put his hand on the knob of the door, opening it. He quickly took a peek inside, and with it all clear, started going in.

"Bring those guys in."

"Why?" Franks asked.

"So nobody sees them if they come walking by."

"If they're not here, they'll know something's up anyway."

"They might just think they walked away somewhere," Thrower said. "Better that than seeing dead guys. Then you know something's up."

"You gonna help?"

"I'm gonna check to make sure no one else is in here."

"Oh. Yeah. You do that, man, I got this. Never thought I'd say dragging dead guys around was the better job, but here we are."

Thrower had to clear the building quickly in order to get eyes on Ames as soon as possible. He saw the steps leading up to the second floor and went over to them. He put his foot on the bottom step to start going up, then stopped when he heard a noise. There was another man walking down the hallway on the first floor. The man was looking at his phone and started talking as Franks dragged one of the bodies in.

The man just assumed it was one of his buddies. "Hey, did you guys ever hear of..." The man looked up, then dropped his phone immediately when he saw Franks' face.

The guard pulled out his gun and stretched his

arm out, ready to use it. Thrower ran up behind him, though, and knocked the gun out of his hands. The guard turned around and tried to throw a punch, but Thrower blocked it, then landed a few punches of his own. Within seconds, both men were suddenly on the floor, with Thrower getting in behind the man's back. Thrower cinched his arm under the man's chin, slowly squeezing the life out of him. It didn't take much longer for the fight to be over.

Once the man was dead, Thrower took his arm off the man's throat and shoved him to the side. Thrower stood up and took another quick look around.

"Remind me never to get on your bad side," Franks said.

"Check out the rest of this floor."

"Me?!"

"I gotta get up there and set up quick."

"What if..." Franks stopped talking as Thrower ran up the steps and disappeared from sight.

Thrower had already taken up more time than he wanted to. He knew Jacobs was getting through the gate right about now, and Thrower wanted to be in position well before Jacobs started talking to Ames.

Franks looked at the hallway to his left and let out a sigh. He gripped his gun, hoping he didn't have to use it. He was OK using it, as long as it wasn't too close of a battle. He wasn't interested in getting into a tussle like Thrower was. If he had a few seconds to line up his shot, he thought he'd be OK. But if it turned into something else, he wasn't sure he could manage it.

Just as he was about to move his legs, Franks stopped, startled at the noise he was hearing upstairs. Thrower had obviously found himself another opponent. As Franks remained stationary, seconds later, a man came violently crashing down the steps, stopping at his permanent resting spot on the first floor. Franks cautiously went over to the man and gently pushed the man's arm with his foot. He wasn't moving. Franks then noticed the knife wound in the man's stomach. He looked up the steps, though he couldn't see Thrower at this point.

"Man, that's one bad mofo. I ain't never having an argument with him."

Franks went and checked out the rest of the floor. There were only a few other rooms down there, but he wasn't too anxious to look in any of them. Luckily, the rest of the floor was empty.

Franks wiped the sweat off his forehead. "Thank the Lord."

He then went up the stairs, though he stopped once he reached the top step. He knew how lethal Thrower was, and Franks wasn't dumb enough to even take a chance on catching him by surprise and risk being on the receiving end of one of his friend's beatings.

"Nate," Franks whispered.

Thrower had already found a spot by a window. Recognizing Franks' voice, he didn't even turn around to answer. "To your right." He stayed focused on his target. He had his rifle out but was careful not to point it out the window and risk being spotted yet.

"Anyone else up here?" Franks asked.

"Not anymore."

"You see Brett yet?"

Thrower nodded in the direction of the window. "Looks like his car's coming in now."

"You want me to do anything?"

"Just stay focused on those steps. Make sure no one comes up behind us. I'll take care of everything out there."

"You got it."

Thrower continued looking out the window, seeing Jacobs' car finally stop just inside the gate. Jacobs made sure he parked where he did to make sure no other cars could come up behind him. If they did, they were hitting a roadblock.

Jacobs sat inside his car for a moment, looking at what was in front of him, which was formidable. There must have been twenty men waiting for him, including Ames. Jacobs noticed him almost right away. Most of the men were standing in front of their cars, which were parked in front of the buildings, but a few were standing behind them.

Jacobs started talking to Gunner, though he never

took his eyes off the dangerous men before him. "You ready for this?"

Gunner let out a deep sounding growl as he leaned forward, looking like he was about to jump out of the car and take his pick of arms to latch onto. He just might have if the window wasn't up.

After a few more seconds of sizing up his opponents, Jacobs finally opened his door. He slowly got out. He stood there, then called for Gunner. Gunner jumped out of the car and immediately started barking.

"Gunner, quiet."

Gunner instantly stopped barking as Jacobs closed the car door. Jacobs wasn't ready to move forward yet. He stood there, looking at all the men waiting for him. Though Gunner was antsy, he sat down by his owner's side. He was ready to pounce at a moment's notice.

Before moving forward, Jacobs spun his head to both sides and peeked behind him, making sure there were no surprises that he wasn't aware of. With everything seeming clear, he moved a few steps, reaching the front of his car. Gunner moved along with him.

As Jacobs moved, so did Ames. Followed by a dozen of his men, he moved about ten feet closer to Jacobs. He was careful not to get too close, though, just in case Jacobs had ideas about going down in a blaze of glory. Ames wasn't going down with him.

"Glad to see you've made it," Ames said.

"Didn't really have much of a choice." Jacobs's eyes continually glanced between Ames' men, making sure none of them pulled a gun that he didn't see.

Ames smiled, proud of his accomplishment. "No, you didn't, did you?" Ames stretched his arms out wide as if he were welcoming Jacobs to a house party. "Well, should we commence with the proceedings?"

"First things first. You call off your men."

Ames shook his head. "That's not how it works. You come forward, then I call them."

Jacobs shook his head. "Nope. Not gonna happen. I'm not doing anything until I hear you call off your men. If not, I'll get back in this car and drive away."

"What makes you think I don't have men out there waiting for you in case you do?"

Jacobs shrugged. "I'll take my chances."

"I believe you would."

"I could also shoot you right now and do the same."

Ames grinned. "Do that and your girlfriend's parents die just the same. Unless they hear my voice in the next five minutes, they have orders to shoot."

"I figured that."

Gunner started growling again, wanting to be let loose, though he wasn't on a leash, anyway. But he always followed Jacobs' commands.

"What do you need him for?" Jacobs asked, looking down briefly at the dog.

"Because he's a vicious mutt that needs to be kept off the street."

"He's not a mutt."

"And because I don't like him, and because he's... well, I could go on for an hour about him too. Let's just say he's right below you on the pecking order. There's no scenario in which he survives this either."

"I take it you're not an animal lover."

"Not when they bite me."

"He hasn't bitten you yet."

"And he'll never get the chance. Luckily, he won't get to see you go down first." Jacobs glared at Ames, wishing he was standing within arm's reach of him, so he could rip his throat out. "Unfortunately, you're gonna see him killed first. But thankfully, you won't have to live with the memory for too long."

"Your mother didn't hold you much as a baby, did she?"

Ames laughed. "You know, that's not the first time I've heard that."

"I'm sure it isn't."

"All right, enough of the talk. It's time to get this over with."

"Make the call. You get nothing until that happens."

"Fine." Ames took out his phone from his pants pocket. He then dialed a number.

"Make sure you say it loud enough for me to hear," Jacobs said.

Ames' man quickly answered. "Cancel the order,"

he said loudly. "It's no longer necessary." Ames then put his phone back in his pocket. "Satisfied?"

"Yeah. I guess that'll do."

"So, are we ready?"

Jacobs shrugged. "Guess as ready as I'll ever be. Let the fun begin."

19

Jacobs stood there for a few seconds, staring at Ames, not moving an inch. Ames was beginning to think he was up to something. At the very least, he was getting him aggravated.

"I made the call," Ames said. "I upheld my part of the bargain. Now it's your turn."

Jacobs put his right hand on top of his head and started scratching. "Well, I'll tell ya... I don't really think I'll feel too badly about taking back my part of it. Especially against you."

"What?"

The shot then rang out. A second later, Ames jolted forward from the impact of the bullet entering the back of his right shoulder. He fell on his hands and knees. As several of Ames' men looked back to figure out where the shot had come from, Jacobs removed his gun and started blasting away.

"Gunner, go!"

Gunner took off like he'd been shot out of a cannon, quickly finding his first victim. Jacobs knelt down by the front of the car and continued firing, keeping an eye on his four-legged friend to make sure he didn't get in over his head. Ames' men diverted their attention between Jacobs and whoever was shooting at them from the other building. It didn't take them very long to determine Thrower's position, considering he mowed down a few more of them after Ames went down.

Confusion and chaos reigned over the next several minutes, Ames' men not sure what they should be doing with their boss down. There was a lot of yelling, some of them pointing at Thrower, some of them pointing at Jacobs, not to mention the couple who were unfortunate enough to be on the receiving end of Gunner's teeth.

They were of course firing back at Jacobs and Thrower, but a few of them wanted to retreat, a few wanted to get their boss and whisk him away, and some wanted to focus on one target over the other. With Ames down, there was no leadership. That was partially how Ames structured his organization. He didn't really want a specific second in command, mostly out of fear that having someone else right under him might cause that person to eventually want to overthrow him.

Most of Ames' men had by now retreated behind

cars, trying to shield themselves from both directions. A couple of the men had broken off and ran in between a couple of the buildings. Their goal was to get in behind whoever was shooting at them from the building and take them out.

They barged into the building, immediately stumbling over the bodies of their dead friends. They were loud enough for Franks to hear them come in, though.

"Looks like we got company, man."

"Switch spots," Thrower said. "You take the window."

Franks rushed over to the window and immediately started firing down below, while Thrower hurried over to the top of the stairs. He got there just in time to see one of the men charging up the steps. Thrower put three rounds into him, causing the man to fall down on top of one of the other ones. Not wanting to keep himself plainly visible, he retreated behind the wall, peeking around it as he waited for the next one to try their luck.

He didn't wait long. Almost immediately, two more of Ames' men rushed up the steps. Thrower jumped out from the wall and instantly locked onto his two targets. His first shot hit the lead man dead in the center of his forehead. As the man fell back, he knocked the man behind him off balance a little, giving Thrower an easy target and without having to duck bullets himself. The man regained his balance just as two bullets ripped into his chest, killing him instantly.

With the two men falling back down the stairs, Thrower retreated again behind the wall, waiting for his next victims to appear. He glanced back at Franks for a moment to see how he was doing.

"How you making out over there?"

Franks fired a couple more rounds, though he also kept ducking the bullets that were flying in his direction. "Uh, you know, just..."

"Are you actually hitting anything?"

"Oh yeah. I'm hitting stuff."

"I mean people!"

"Oh. Well, that I'm not sure. I mean, I may have winged someone."

"Fantastic."

Out in front, Jacobs was staying busy, alternating between trying to kill members of Ames' entourage, and keeping Gunner safe from men trying to kill him. As the minutes went by, slowly but surely, Ames' men began to dwindle. Eventually, there was less than ten, and rather than sticking it out and fighting a battle that they were clearly losing, they decided to get out of there.

"What about the boss?!" one of them said.

"Leave him! He's dead, anyway!"

"I think he's still breathing."

Even though a couple of them didn't want to bother, three of them went over to Ames' body and dragged him into the back seat of one of their vehicles. He was still alive, though he was in bad shape, bleeding all over the place. Once their boss was in the car, the driver stepped on the gas. They started driving towards Jacobs, though his car was blocking their way out.

Since ramming the car didn't seem like their best option, the car quickly turned directions. They sped to the right of the buildings, looking to get out the back way. Jacobs kept firing his gun, hoping to take out a few more of them on the way out, or shoot the driver, making him crash the car.

With no one else on the ground, Gunner retreated back to his position next to his owner. Jacobs kept firing at the car as it rounded the edge of the building on the right. Even Franks was taking his shots at the vehicle, though he didn't have much chance of actually doing any damage.

As the car disappeared from sight, Franks stopped firing, then turned toward his partner. "Well, looks like that's it. We did it."

"They're gone?" Thrower asked.

"Yep." Franks looked out the window again, observing all the bodies that were now on the ground. "Man, that's a lot of dead people down there."

"Don't feel bad for them. They brought it on themselves."

"Oh, no doubt, man, I ain't feeling bad for them. Still a lot of bodies, though. Guess we should hightail it out of here."

"Brett out there?"

"Yeah, he and the pooch are still alive and kicking."

"Looks like this has been a success."

"Well, as long as Tiffany got her parents out, it's a success." Franks saw Jacobs by his car, getting on the phone. He assumed he was checking out the same thing. "Let's get out of here now, huh?"

Franks followed Thrower down the steps, observing that he was moving pretty good. Once they stepped foot on the first floor, Franks pointed to Thrower's leg.

"Hey, the leg don't look like it's bothering you too much."

Thrower looked down at it. "Oh. Yeah. Forgot all about it. It'll take more than that to keep me down."

Suddenly, a shot rang through the air. Franks jolted forward, with Thrower putting out his arms to catch him. Another shot was fired, narrowly missing the both of them. Thrower gently tossed his friend to the side and located the shooter. The two men engaged in battle, each getting a couple of shots off. Thrower's aim was more accurate, though, and he promptly took care of the man.

Thrower stood there for a few moments, moving in every direction, making sure there were no other threats. Then he heard someone else coming by the front door. He pointed his gun in that direction, seeing Jacobs stick his head in quickly, before pulling it back out.

"You good?" Jacobs asked.

"Eddie's hit!" Thrower put his gun away, then checked on Franks' condition.

Jacobs and Gunner ran through the door, instantly locating Franks on the floor. He was lying face down, but he wasn't moving. Jacobs put his hand on Franks' back, checking out the damage. He thought it strange they weren't seeing any blood yet.

"Eddie?"

Franks didn't answer. Jacobs moved his finger along Franks' back, trying to find the bullet hole. He then shifted the bulletproof vest around that Franks was wearing, noticing that the bullet hadn't gone through. He breathed a huge sigh of relief, looking at Thrower who saw the same thing.

"Eddie," Jacobs said.

"Just turn me over guys," Franks replied. "Just let me look at you's one last time."

Jacobs chuckled. Thrower laughed. But they helped Franks over onto his back. Even Gunner let out a bark.

"Don't worry, little guy, I'll be waiting for you up there with a bone or something."

"Eddie," Jacobs said, wanting to break the news to him that he wasn't dying.

"I know. I know. It's bad. My back feels like it's on fire."

"Eddie, it's not that bad."

"Don't sugarcoat things, man. I can take it. We had a good run, though, didn't we? Took on all comers."

Jacobs cleared his throat. "Yeah. A pretty good run."

"Wish I was gonna be there to see the end of it."

"You will be."

Franks put his hand on Jacobs' forearm and tapped him a couple of times. "It's OK, man, it's OK. I'm not scared or nothing."

"You're not, huh?"

"No. You know, it's kinda funny. I always assumed that it was gonna hurt real bad. But I don't really feel nothing. I guess my body's numb or something."

Jacobs looked at Thrower and shook his head. "You don't feel anything because you're not shot."

"Dude, it's OK. I know it's tough to lose the people you care about. But I want you to move on from this. Promise me that. I'm at peace with everything. I want you to be too."

Jacobs looked at him and continued to shake his head. "Eddie, listen to what I'm saying. You're not shot. That's why you don't feel anything. Because your vest took the bullet. It didn't penetrate."

Franks' eyes widened, looking like they were about to jump out of his head. "What?"

Jacobs smiled and laughed. "You're not shot. You're not dying. You're fine."

Franks put his hands on his chest, feeling around. "I'm not shot?"

Jacobs shook his head. "Nope."

Franks looked at Thrower. "Is he kidding me, man? Because if he is, it's a cruel, cruel joke."

Thrower confirmed the result. "He's not kidding. You're really not shot."

Franks then swiftly got to his feet and jumped into the air. He let out a high-pitched scream. "Oh, thank the Lord! I'm not shot!" Then, as the shock started to wear off, he let out a grunt that indicated he was in pain. He put his hand on his back. "Ooh, kind of sore back there."

"Yeah, that sometimes happens," Jacobs said. "You can still feel the impact without the result."

"Hey, whatever, it's better than the alternative."

"It certainly is."

"Hey, man, that's kind of mean of you two. Letting me think I was shot and all, just letting me lay there without telling me nothing."

Jacobs looked at Thrower, both of them throwing their hands up.

"What about Tiffany's parents?" Thrower asked.

"They're good," Jacobs answered. "Just called her before I came in here. She said everything's good. Bucky even arrested the two guys that were there. Criminal records, had guns, so they're going away for a while."

"What about the other two guards?"

"Oh, they found them in the trunk of a car. They'll be OK."

"Seems as if everything worked out in our favor."

"Yeah, seems like."

Gunner then started barking at them.

"The pooch is right, guys," Franks said. "Let's get out of here and save the celebrating for another day. Besides, I got a warm bath calling for me right now."

"Surprised you're not taking a trip to Lucy and Deb's," Jacobs said.

Franks snapped his fingers, then pointed at him. "Now you're talking! Now you're talking!"

The team walked out of the building and headed for the car, hopeful that they'd never have to deal with Ames again.

20

Mallette was led into the room, seeing his new lawyer walk into the room at the same time. Berry put his arm up, almost as if he were trying to get spotted in a large crowd. He was excited at the information he had to present to his client today. He hurried over to the table, starting to unpack his stuff as Mallette made his way over there.

Mallette had a stoic look on his face, still not really expecting much. But he supposed it was better than spending the time in his cell. At least it gave him something different to look at.

"I've got it," Berry excitedly said. "I've got it."

"You've got what?"

Berry put his finger in the air. "I've got the thing I think is going to get you out of here."

"Oh?" Mallette didn't sound nearly as excited as the lawyer did. Probably the result of being led down this road too many times before, only to have his hopes smashed. "You do, huh?"

Berry couldn't wipe the smile off his face. He was confident he was getting his client out of jail. "Yes." He looked down at one of the papers in front of him, turned it around, and slid it over to his client.

Mallette looked at it, not really seeing the relevance. "So?"

"Don't you see?"

"No."

Berry reached over and pointed to the paragraph that was the most interesting. "There it is. Right there."

"I'm not seeing it."

"Well, clearly your rights were violated. There's no question in my mind that's a violation of your rights."

"So?"

"So I'm gonna start petitioning in a few days to get you out of here early."

"And what are the chances of that?"

"I think they're very, very good. Extremely good. Not to get your hopes up too much, but I think you can start counting the days until you're released."

"You'll forgive me if I don't sound overly enthused. It's just that I've heard all of this before."

"Oh, believe me, I wouldn't be telling you this unless I was very sure of the outcome."

"The proof will be in the pudding, as they say."

∾

Franks came into the room of Jacobs' new place, finding Jacobs and Tiffany sitting on the couch close together. Thrower was in a chair across from them, and Gunner was on the floor.

"So what do you think of it?" Franks asked, holding his arms out to his side and turning his head.

Jacobs looked around. "It's not bad."

"Not bad? Not bad, he says. Tell me this isn't even better than your last place. Tell me it's not."

"It's OK."

Franks' shoulders slumped. "It's OK. What do you think, Tiff?"

Tiffany looked at Jacobs and smiled, then answered the question. "It's very nice, Eddie."

"Thank you. At least there's someone here who appreciates my genius."

"You just found a house," Jacobs said. "You didn't perform brain surgery."

"Be nice, Brett," Tiffany said. "Be appreciative of what Eddie's done."

Jacobs laughed and scratched his forehead. "OK. Thank you, Eddie. This is really lovely."

"I know you're mocking me now, so now I'm only speaking to her." Franks turned his attention to Tiffany. "Since you're the only one here with manners, I'd just like to say thank you for treating and talking to me properly."

"It really is nice," Tiffany replied. "There's a lot more room." Gunner barked, causing Tiffany to laugh.

"And yes, Gunner likes that there's more room in the backyard for him too."

"Well, you're all welcome." He then looked at Jacobs. "Except for you."

Jacobs put his hand over his mouth to try to prevent him from laughing. "Well, it did take you long enough. I mean, spending a week on your couch is not that comfortable."

"Is it my fault these things take time? I could've gotten you some dump, you know. And it's lucky for you that she's here, or else I might have. If it wasn't for her, I still might."

"Are you two staying here together permanently?" Thrower asked.

Jacobs and Tiffany looked at each other, neither quite sure of the answer. It wasn't something they had really discussed. They were each kind of just going with the flow.

"Uh, I don't know," Tiffany said. "Are we?"

"Um..." He then shrugged. "I don't know. I guess we'd have to figure out how safe things are out there."

"Yeah, what's the word on Ames?" Thrower asked.

"Nothing," Franks answered. "There ain't no word. Nobody seems to know nothing. He hasn't popped up in any hospitals that I can tell."

"That's good, isn't it?" Tiffany asked.

"Well, could be good. Too early to tell yet."

"I don't understand. Why isn't it good? That would mean he's not getting treated for injuries, isn't it?"

"Well, like I said, it's too early to tell. Could be that he's got his own doctors, not exactly above ground, if you know what I mean."

"Wouldn't you have heard something, though?"

"Well, maybe. Maybe not. Depends how buttoned up they got everything."

"What about cemeteries, death notices, things like that?" Jacobs asked.

"That's the other thing. I can't find anything that indicates he's being treated for something, but I can't find anything that says he's dead either. So without there being any type of word in either direction... I just can't say for sure yet."

"I guess that solves it for now."

"Solves what?" Tiffany said.

"Until I know for sure that it's safe for you to go back to your own apartment, I'd feel better if you stayed here with me," Jacobs said.

"Talk about torture," Franks said, looking at Tiffany. "I mean for you, not him."

Tiffany looked over at Thrower. "What about you, Nate? What are your plans now?"

Thrower shrugged. "I dunno. Don't have anything else lined up at the moment."

"Why don't you stick around here for a while?"

Thrower smiled. "I just might do that. Plus, without knowing exactly what Ames' status is, I shouldn't really leave yet until I know the job is finished."

"Great. Do you have a place to stay?"

"Uh, I got him a little something," Franks said. "If he wants it. Not quite as big as this place, but it's cozy enough for one guy. You're already paid up for a month."

"Well, guess that settles it," Thrower said. "Looks like I'm sticking around for a little while."

"What about it?" Jacobs asked, nudging Tiffany in the arm.

"What about what?"

"You never replied to my statement."

"Which was?"

"I'd feel better if you stayed here a while. At least until we find out what happened to Ames. What do you think?"

She smiled, then leaned over and kissed him. "I can think of worse places to be."

ABOUT THE AUTHOR

Mike Ryan is a USA Today Bestselling Author. He lives in Pennsylvania with his wife, and four children. He's the author of the bestselling Silencer Series, as well as many others. Visit his website at www.mikeryanbooks.com to find out more about his books, and sign up for his newsletter to be notified of new releases. You can also interact with Mike via Facebook, and Instagram.

ALSO BY MIKE RYAN

Continue with the next book in The Eliminator Series, The Return.

Other books:

The Silencer Series

The Extractor Series

The Brandon Hall Series

The Cain Series

The Ghost Series

A Dangerous Man

The Last Job

The Crew